GW01191334

LIF

With best
wishes
from
Anthee

Anthea Church 10/2/2025

By the same author

Non-fiction
Angels
Invocations
The Arts of Life
Inner Beauty
Inner Space
Padma's Story
Madhuban
The Poetry of Teaching

Fiction
Fire-fly
Sleeping with Mozart

ANTHEA CHURCH

LIFTMAN

A Novel

First published in the UK in 2023 by Shakspeare Editorial, UK

ISBN 978-1-7392549-5-7 (paperback)
ISBN 978-1-7392549-6-4 (ebook)

Cover design Cali Mackrill
Typesetting www.ShakspeareEditorial.org

This novel was written twenty-five years after I formally left a community resembling the one described in these pages. Readers who are still a part of that community, as well as former members, will recognise some references to its rules, customs and setting. However, all events and characters described are fictional. Any resemblance to actual persons is coincidental.

To the memory of
Ranjana Patel and her brother Sharad

INDIA 1990

1

A far from unusual sight in India, in the rising heat of the morning: a young man sitting hunched and solitary at the foot of the steps leading up to The Sunshine Hotel, Ahmedabad. He could be a beggar, a holy man, a sadhu. Or he could be a tourist, some hopeful hippy out of England or the US, resting up before starting on the last leg of his hitchhiker trail up north.

And yet he was all and none of these. By his casual clothing and backpack, he was a travelling Westerner; by the colour of his skin and gauntness of his body he was Indian; and by the unworldly look in his eye – if you could get close enough to see it – there was something of the wayward saint about him.

Kasper Chaudhury was well aware of all such dualities. There was a wallet full of banknotes on his person and a pouch of rupees in his pocket. He was travelling from his home and he was travelling towards his home. And he was, at the same time, both with and without expectation.

A sharp shotgun-crack startled him out of his reverie and, peering along the dusty road trailing out of town towards the plain beyond, he could see a white Hindustan Ambassador lurching and backfiring in his direction.

Realising it was the taxi that had been ordered for him, he watched as it rattled its way across three redundant roundabouts and rose to his feet as the vehicle pulled up and the driver's window went down.

It wasn't the battered state of the car or the dire spluttering and gasping issuing from its engine that made him recoil, or even the sight of the driver's sweat-smeared face with the gold tooth in the nicotine-shrunken gums. No, it was the unholy stink coming from inside the car that brought him close to retching even as the driver looked up to sound him out:

'Mr Chaudhury – for Aramani?'

'Yes.'

'Quite some journey.'

'So can you take me?'

'Yes, no – your choice.'

By the pained look on Kasper's face, the driver could see he was in two minds.

'So it's the smell that is providing you with bother? Alas, there is a small cargo I must carry.' The driver pointed to the back seat where a large sack lay on its side. 'It's a special spice, very delicate in cooking but not so good to smell'

'Hing – yes, I know.'

'Ah, then you know also that you will soon get used to it.'

For the first couple of hours, Kasper fought back the stench, trying to doze, telling himself that hing was a way of preparing to re-encounter his old home whose combination of smells had been so hard to summon while away. But he was without the control he had once had over his body. And when the taxi rounded a bend too fast, he yanked down the window only just in time.

This spewing of guts seemed far from auspicious, the thought occurring to him that it might be a message from The Philosophy, which taught that endless recollecting only weighed you down. But it was too late for regret; they were now more than halfway to Aramani.

'Please, I need water.'

An hour passed before a couple of petrol pumps came into view. The driver swung the car in a vertiginous arc, skidded to a halt and got out. Kasper followed, standing for a few moments, back pressed against the warmth of the car door. Then he bought a bottle of water from a café, took out his pad of sugar paper and began drawing: the shoulder of a man he had met in Amsterdam; a memory of a Van Gogh sketch; a flight of steps; the block-pencilled grey of an elevator door; and close by, two boys who were fooling about in the heat.

Just as he was beginning to relax, a yell sounded out. He spun round and saw one of the boys fall and hit his head against the pavement. He must have allowed his chair to tilt too far backwards. And it was then, in a moment of unexpected bleakness, that Kasper longed to be taken to Aramani's infirmary and given a remedy both mild and precise. But he wasn't the boy who had fallen; it wasn't his head that was bleeding; and he was no longer a child.

Life upon life seemed to pass before the driver finally ambled back to his vehicle. No words were exchanged

3

and, as the engine revved, Kasper concentrated only on keeping his breathing even.

'When we're half a mile from Aramani, please drop me off. I'll walk the rest of the way.'

'Aramani. That's a hole of a place if you ask me.'

Six months earlier, his father had used the same word: 'Kasper, I beg of you, never set foot in that hole again.' Unlike the taxi driver, who made a good living out of delivering both travellers and hing to the place he bad-mouthed, his father had had good reason to speak in such terms. But while a person's words often gain weight after death, his father's warning had died with him.

The tight-knit community in the Aravali mountains, where Kasper had lived from the age of seven, had never been far from his mind. In twisted versions of itself, sometimes bewitchingly sweet, others coercive and bullish, dreams of the place had alternately calmed and disrupted his nights. Just after his father's funeral, Aramani had come to him in an image of such warmth that on an afternoon in late January he had walked into the London rain, found the nearest travel agent and booked a flight to Ahmedabad.

One way.

2

The half-mile walk to the village on the outskirts of Aramani should have taken under fifteen minutes, given that Kasper had intended to move fast. If he stopped to look, the questions would begin: why had he left, why was he back, how would they react to his return...?

What he most yearned for was a combination of comfort and clarity; to use his old home both to heal himself of sorrow and to gain an objective view of his childhood – and so also his future.

> *If you ever lose your way, return to the last place you felt safe and start again from there.*

With this maxim from Aramani's Philosophy in mind he reached the village. Here, the soft steam of cow dung, the ashy fragrance of incense and the vibrant fabrics hanging on rails in roadside stores confused his intentions. As did the burst of song from a group of scampering children, sleek black hair plaited tight and neat, dresses pressed, parcelled schoolbooks swinging from red-cardiganed arms.

It was here in the village that he had collected the Elders' laundry, talked daily to the donkey. Here, his friend Amba had stolen a motorbike. Here, he had been happy...

Why had he abandoned it, then?

To fight the mix of sweetness and guilt, he pushed himself forwards. Beside the cricket pitch, the turning to the marketplace, on to the road from which makeshift steps dropped down into Aramani itself.

On his way, he crossed the dried-out crease of a riverbed. As a sixteen-year-old, he had looked down on the families who made their ramshackle homes there. Now he regarded them with respect. They weren't burdened with The Philosophy, didn't care if they ate holy food or paid their respects to a deity. They were content in their own circle of love, stoically surviving the devastation caused annually by the August monsoons.

Approaching Aramani's gates with their vivid posters promising welcome and enlightenment, Kasper finally managed to steady his step. He was keen not to be spotted yet wanted to see everything.

The tailors' quarters were locked for the afternoon, workers dozing on cane bedsteads in the shade of the khejri trees. Beyond their closed door, another, to the darkroom where Amba developed photographs of the Elders. Then the carpenter's workshop, also empty, although the door was open, a pile of chopped up bedsteads in view. Finally, the steps that led up to the kitchen.

Above him, trolleys of tea were being pushed in the direction of the outdoor dining room.

The dining room: that place of joy where he had eaten freely and fully, talked and laughed and watched the monkeys leap from roof to roof... All attempts to control his emotions collapsed as his boyhood rushed to embrace him: Hey Kasper, come and stir the milk with us, drink with us, tell us a joke, listen to the cricket.

Had any of the Elders seen him, they would have spoken with just such warmth. He was at the heart of their world, gone for a little, but home again now.

However far away, everyone returns in the end.

As he approached the courtyard, Aramani's central meeting place, the sun struck his face as if he had walked out onto a set: white light, jasmine, bougainvillea, the smell of freshly pressed clothes, sweets, fruit… so that once more he concluded that, whatever the flaws either in Aramani or himself, the place had a power no one could dispute. Certainly not a taxi driver, although his reference to the place as a hole was disturbing, as was the skyline broken by the two white domes of a sophisticated new building. He wondered if the kites still wheeled through the sky as they had in the past or perhaps they, too, had been driven away.

To one side of the courtyard, Viraj sat on a gold lacquered chair. Among the most respected of the Elders, his position was advertised by the spotlessly clean churidars, kurta top and cream flannel waistcoat, uniform which Kasper, too, had been proud to wear from the age of sixteen.

'Viraj.'

The old man stood up, stretched out his hand and spoke Kasper's name. The address was so gentle that it drew Kasper into the same calmness it had when, as a boy, he had lost either footing or discipline.

Seated again, Viraj beckoned to a sister.

'Have Kasper's room made ready. He'll need to wash.'

Kasper suddenly wondered if he smelt of hing but didn't dare ask. In any case, he was cross with Aramani for being so fastidious. How it crippled life! All the rules about bathing, the round upon round of classes which themselves moved in circles, the same ideas repeated over and over; the instruction against laughing with your mouth open, saying anything unkind, trivial, worldly…

He had forgotten, too, how Viraj had only to signal and the machinery of Aramani's impeccable hospitality was instantly set in motion. But that was a part of the strangeness of the place that, away from it, you could neither forget it nor quite recall the exact power by which it worked.

In his room, all was as before: the bed narrow, pillow flat, sheets white-grey and tightly tucked in. Later he would unpack, set each possession in its place: alarm clock on the cabinet by the bed; sketchpad and drawing pencils on the desk; on shelves lined with pages torn from back copies of The Indian Times, his clothes. The thought of these moves relaxed him, as if in laying out his life he would shed the weight of the cloud that had gathered about him during his five years away.

Visitors to Aramani always spoke of the pleasure of arrival. Whatever their stay brought, whether tests of the conscience or challenges to their stamina, the first feelings they described were those of order and relief.

Kasper switched on the fan and, lying on the bed, stared at its arms swishing the afternoon air, then at the photograph of Aramani's founder, Gayan, which hung in a gilt frame above the desk.

During his five years in the West, he had often longed for a copy of that picture. Now the face smiled and he thought: it's you who's arranged for me to be back in my old room. And he was grateful. For the room would give him a contained space from which to reassess what Aramani had once been to him, and what it now meant.

As if to begin he fished sketchpad from rucksack and went over to the desk where, as a teenager, he had painstakingly drawn diagrams to illustrate The Philosophy, or just absorbed himself in drawing.

But it wasn't the right thing.

> *On arrival, change out of your worldly clothes, take a bath and prepare to greet the Elders.*

> *But I don't live here anymore.*

Two truths in combat.

4

Across Aramani's campus phones began ringing. Viraj called Anouka who summoned Kasper's first teacher and friend, the photographer Amba, who ran to wake Banhi, the elderly keeper of the fruit store. Finally, a brother Kasper had never met walked into his room without knocking.

'Anouka wants you.'

'Later.'

'She says now.'

'Well, she'll have to wait.'

Sharp in his rebuff, Kasper was annoyed to discover himself unable to ignore the summons. Agitated, he went into the bathroom, crouched to fill a bucket with warm water and poured it over himself. Having neither soap nor towel, he walked dripping into the darkened bedroom, dried himself on a blanket and dressed in the only pair of white kurtas he had with him. Although now accustomed to Western clothing, he was still plagued by the idea that bright colours signalled confusion, while in white you could be neutral and so think life through clearly.

On his first sight of Anouka for five years – the sheer beam of the woman with her brilliant white hair and piercing brown eyes, the sense of her being so free of all brushes with the world – Kasper was overcome by shame.

'You look ill.'

This observation hurt. How dare she comment on his travel-tired body when what she was really saying was that he'd become weak, that the muscles of his soul were flaccid?

'I won't be staying long, Anouka, but I grew up here. I have a right to come back.'

Her face opened into a smile and she pressed a sweet of crushed almonds and cardamom into the palm of his hand. Her touch was precious with love, reminding him of the hundreds of times he had run to her as a boy and chattered while she was dressing or plaiting her hair. She was a large woman, as different from his slim, blonde mother as it was possible for a woman to be; he had been fascinated by her bulk and what it was made of. When dressed in her sari, she had the look of an iceberg while her face was warm and nut-brown. Even her bathroom was pristine. Her hairbrush, the hairpins on the shelf by the basin, her comb and the sharp square of her soap had always made him want to run back to his room for his sketchpad.

On a shelf in her cupboard, she kept a selection of silver boxes. One day he had asked her to show him what was inside them. Her frown told him *no*. 'They're rewards for students who work hard', she had said, pinching his cheeks then cramming his hands full of sweets and announcing that since he was only a child he should just keep smiling and eat, even though The Philosophy ruled against such freedom. Now, in this moment of return, he felt an urge to bury himself in her lap like the child he had been. The impulse died at her next words: 'Eat in the Elders' dining room. Come to the classes. The tailor will make you new kurtas.'

But it was too late for him to sit in a class about the nature of the soul, or God, or the Great Tree of Life. Nor did he wish to be treated as someone special and eat with the Elders.

'In your letter, you offered to operate the lift again. Rest for a few days first. And stay as long as you like. This is your home. But cause us no trouble, Kasper.'

Then a phone blared into the whiteness, the warmth drained out of her face and she lost all interest in his presence. Watching this helped Kasper compose himself, as did the memory that once, when Anouka had decided to remain in silence for a week, she had emerged from her room to announce that she had checked the state of her soul and concluded that, after thirty-five years' work, it was as 'flawless as a diamond'.

The truth of the matter was that, for the most part, if they loved a person, the residents of Aramani ignored the rule of non-attachment. Kasper, they loved deeply, and the letter announcing his return had excited them.

Viraj had made arrangements for a meal of welcome. Knowing that Kasper liked palak paneer and stuffed rotis, he had instructed these to be served along with other delicacies and, to finish, a brand of jasmine tea provided by a visitor from Hong Kong, which had since become a favourite. Also a cake.

They waited half an hour and when Kasper didn't turn up they tackled the food on their own. An atmosphere of repressed hurt took the pleasure from their eating.

The cake was never brought in.

After dinner, they dispersed: Viraj, to his room, where he sat for an hour behind a newspaper; Anouka to a discussion about the opening of a studio in Goa; and Amba, Kasper's childhood friend and first teacher, to his tool shed, where he wrestled with a bicycle chain.

Meanwhile, seated at his desk, Kasper broke one of the strictest of Aramani's rules by eating food not prepared on its premises. Leafing through the sketches he had made during the journey, he wolfed down the remains of two soggy chapattis, then rice and dhal he had bought in a cheap plastic container from the hotel in Ahmedabad.

5

Waking was a shock. Day after day in Europe, he had come to in a sweat, thinking himself back in Aramani. As often, he had woken not knowing where he was. To sit up and see his old room about him, with all its familiar colours and shapes, filled him with confusion because he knew, as if the thought had been dropped into his mind by Gayan himself, that the place could never be as it had been.

He went over to the cupboard where he had hung his clothes the night before and took out the silk kimono Hanneke had given him one summer in Holland. It didn't belong in this celibate room, but he put it on anyway, as if he needed it to help him stay close to his body, which seemed these days so often to convey the truth more clearly than words.

Six to ten Elders were gathered in the dining room for breakfast. When Kasper slipped in beside them, some turned to smile.

Do not talk when the body is being fed.

But joy made them careless. As if longing to take him

into themselves and re-make him, they bombarded him with questions: where had he been; what had he been doing; did he still have a 'special friend'; where did he live; why had he lost so much weight; by what means had he travelled; had he been shown the new buildings; and when would they see him in the early morning class?

Some questions he answered. Yes, he'd had a good journey. Yes, he'd noticed the two white domes, what were they? No, he wouldn't be coming to any classes. Yet.

He despised himself for the yet, but it was quicker to lie.

Behind him, at a table in the corner, Banhi, the fruit-keeper, shovelled rice and dhal into her toothless mouth. When Kasper turned to smile at her and she didn't look up, he scraped his chair back fast and went to crouch down beside her. Her bulk was warm against his shoulder but, searching the wide expanse of her face, he saw that her eyes were milky and vacant.

'It's Kasper!' someone shouted at her.

He tightened his hold; in response she laughed, as if she had no idea who he was or, if she had, he was merely the source of a sensation that gave pleasure.

Soon after his first arrival in Aramani, Kasper had been given the task of helping Banhi sort the fruit. In the eyes of the boy she was ancient, but she must only have been middle-aged then. He had loved the way she had looked like a potato – ugly and scraped clean, hair drawn back into a bun that accentuated the bumps on her head. Smelling of oranges and darkness, whenever she saw him she would call out his name then set him some small task.

Occasionally she would come into the fruit store just to tease him by rearranging the oranges, apples, bunches of grapes so that he thought he had made a mistake. A training, perhaps, in community life which, preaching equality, was rigidly hierarchical. Senior, junior; right, wrong; insider, visitor. A place of pairs like the kites that flew in circles above it.

Then there was the day her mouth had caved in. He must have been eight or so when she had taken him to collect a delivery of spices from the small town at the foot of the mountain. She sat next to the driver; Kasper leant out of the jeep like a sailor on a trapeze, staring up at the sky and down into ravines and valleys, lush green after the monsoon. The inside of the jeep smelt damp, the dirty towel over the back of the driver's seat and the little statue of an Indian god hanging from his mirror seeming to Kasper to come from another world entirely. And from then on, he noticed the difference between the villagers' holy relics and the equivalent artefacts in Aramani; how the little figurines of Krishna that popped up everywhere in shops lacked Aramani's gleam.

An hour or so into the journey, Banhi began singing. Then, as they rounded a bend, she wound down the window. Too late. With as simple as an exhalation, she vomited, her dentures flying out of the window into the valley beneath. He imagined small sails fixed to the gums opening like parachutes, and when he sat up, he saw Banhi's mouth had turned into a puckered O.

She made nothing of the loss and, once at the fruit market, bargained her way through her purchases with as much rigour as if she had a mouthful of fangs to frighten off fraudsters.

Brushing his teeth after his first breakfast back, he wondered why nobody had paid to replace hers. But then, in Aramani nothing was like England: no proper toothbrushes, no dentists, no sitting rooms, no TVs, no days in a classroom, no books, no homework...

More than any of these there was an absence of explanation. So that on a wintery day in the second month of 1970 when he had just celebrated his seventh birthday, no one had knelt before him and laid out in clear terms why he should be lifted out of the English life he had been born into and transported to this new land.

All he knew was what he saw: the back seat of a car, an airport, suitcases, a plane and, beside him, his mother. Being so young, he had enjoyed the sensation of flight, the wide expanse of sky, the dishes of fruit, triangles of toast and capsules of jam brought to him on a tray. He had no idea why his father wasn't beside him, but there was another man who helped him with the ring pull on a lemonade can and an air hostess who had clicked his safety belt neat and tight.

Once in Aramani, the question of where he was and why had been instantly hushed by the sight of Gayan at the gate, there as if summoned only by thought: a tall, slim figure, stretching out his arms to hold mother and son in an embrace so warm that the length and strangeness of the journey were instantly forgotten.

They had been taken to a twin room where his mother disappeared into the bathroom, leaving Kasper to wait. Re-emerging in a towel, she walked, head tilted to one side, combing her blonde hair over one shoulder and plaiting it. Then she lifted from her case a length of white cloth, a sari in gauzy cotton, and he watched as she wound it around her until she was no longer his mother but a cross between stranger and ghost. The figure passed him a white collarless shirt and a pair of cotton trousers.

'Put them on.'

'But they're pyjamas.'

She knelt down beside him.

'This is where we're going to be, Kasper. You'll be happy. I promise. You'll have to follow some rules, but you'll be happy.'

'What rules?'

She pointed to a garishly illustrated leaflet on the desk.

'It says you have to have lots of baths and you have two fathers. How can you have two fathers? Why isn't Daddy with us? And look, it says you can't eat onions.'

'Don't worry about any of that now.'

'Why can't you eat onions?'

'Forget about onions.'

Staring at the leaflet, Kasper had burst into tears.

Night took his sorrow and over the days that followed he slowly began to enjoy a new sense of freedom. Sometimes, he sat with the residents in their Philosophy classes; other days, he stayed in bed, filling page after page of his sketchpad with drawings. The best of it was that he didn't have to go to school, that horrible brick prison where he had been chivvied to read and write when all he had wanted to do was paint.

Often he'd run down the hill to see Gayan. Unlike a

headmaster's office, there was no need to knock or ask for an appointment. On approach, he would simply call out in one or two of the only Hindi phrases he knew. He liked the rounded sound of its words, and soon he could more or less understand what the adults about him were saying, while he could read and write English no better than a six-year-old.

In the photos of Gayan, the man's eyes were heavily made-up, but in person they were deep blue and clear. Once, Kasper had asked him why there was a picture of him in every room and why his eyelids were painted silver. 'Why, why, why,' Gayan had teased, then explained that he couldn't be everywhere at once, so the picture served as a reminder.

In the face of such magic, Kasper quickly forgot his father. As long as his mother was close by, he was content to treat Aramani as a huge outdoor classroom where lessons came to him through the wind in the khejri trees, the howl of wild dogs scavenging the mountain paths or the occasional sharp word from a resident.

The best of the day was morning. Instead of rushing for a bus in the tight grey of blazer and trousers, he would run the entire length and breadth of Aramani in his pyjamas. Sometimes he took his sketchpad and copied one of the cartoon versions of The Philosophy that were plastered over every spare wall, so that you couldn't turn round without a slogan hitting you in the face.

Once, he had stolen a pastry brush and beaker from the kitchen and, stretching up to a poster, painted the fingernails of an officious-looking Elder bright blue. After that, he moved on to a diagram of a car, its driver labelled THE SOUL, the car THE BODY. Here, he traced a thick black line round the wheels and gave the driver an extra ear.

Occasionally, he wandered into the milk kitchens to help make the tea. While what he enjoyed most was to dash across the flat roofs of the accommodation blocks as if, with a special power at his heels, he could fly.

Mid-morning, Kasper would hang out with Amba, the slim, buck-toothed photographer, lifting flimsy reels of film out of some foul-smelling solution and hanging them on what looked to him like a washing line. At the front of the room was a projector on which he showed Kasper the pictures he had developed the day before.

Amba was meant only to take photos of the Elders or to make postcards of self-improving slogans, which Gayan liked to sell at the kiosk just inside Aramani's front gates.

'What shall we have today?' he would ask Kasper. 'Which slogan do you like best?'

'Don't eat onions. Anouka is fat. Kala is fatter. Boom boom boom!'

And Amba would laugh for Kala was an Elder neither of them liked. Middle-aged and robust, Kasper often fell foul of her, particularly when he sneezed, a noise she found offensive, while for Amba she seemed to feel unreserved disapproval.

'Why are they all so fat?'

'I don't know. You're not fat. I'm not fat,' said Amba, who was often refused second helpings at meals on the grounds that his first course had been ample.

'And why can't I eat onions?'

Like his mother, Amba told Kasper to forget onions, they weren't important. Then he lifted the small boy onto a sack-covered box in front of a sheet and told him to stand like an English policeman, hands behind his back.

'I'll take a photo of you. Then I'll paint your eyelids silver like Gayan's, and when you go back to London, you can show them how beautiful you were when you were in Aramani.'

'I'm never going back to London. I'd have to go to school if I was in London.'

'You should go to school. You need qualifications to be free.'

'I'm free here.'

'Maybe, maybe not. Let's take another picture of you sitting cross-legged like a guru. Look, you can wear this.' And Amba had placed a small velvet cap on the boy's head, given him a notebook and told him to lean on one arm as if writing something profound.

Kasper drew a picture of an aeroplane and the photo was taken.

'Look!' Amba cried as the image shimmied into focus.

'You have it,' said Kasper.

'No, it's yours.'

'I've got no one to give it to.'

'I'll look after it for you. You look sweet in my cap.'

Another morning, when Amba was late, Kasper lay under the narrow daybed at one end of the darkroom and waited. When Amba finally turned up, instead of beginning work, he too lay down. Within seconds he was snoring. Kasper remained stock-still for a few minutes, then stuck his finger through one of the slats in the bedstead, poking Amba in the back. His friend sat up fast. Crawling into the light, Kasper hit his head on the side of the bed.

'Serves you right,' said Amba. 'You should know you can't get away with anything in Aramani.'

The anger in his voice made Kasper anxious. In those days, Aramani was an easy-going heaven of openings and chances. There were no refusals, no rules he abided by. He had little idea of words that shouldn't be uttered or sins not committed, so that when Amba told him that he should never under any circumstances come into the darkroom on his own, he felt as if he had stumbled against an electric fence.

6

If Amba wasn't in his darkroom, he could be found in a small shed outside Aramani's gates, in which he made what he called his rainbow medicine. For this, he would place large jars on a wall, fill them with water, use different coloured overlays as lids from his darkroom and leave the jars in the sun, claiming that the water absorbed the power of each colour differently. Sometimes Kasper would pretend he was ill, just to see which colour water Amba might recommend.

'You don't need my water,' he said. 'It's for the Elders. Anouka needs green. Gayan, every different colour. So many people ask him for help. He takes all their problems into his own body.'

'What about Mama?'

Amba sat on the wall next to him.

'I don't know her well enough, but working for Viraj isn't easy. She would benefit from brown.'

'I can't give her brown.' Kasper pulled a face then whispered in Amba's ear.

'No, Kasper, you don't understand. It's not that the water is brown, it's that it's filled with the energy of the earth.'

'Is that in The Philosophy?' Kasper asked, not meaning to hurt, only wanting attention.

Amba said nothing and, for the first time, Kasper realised that his friend had his own ways that didn't entirely fall in with the thinking taught in Aramani. Not that he cared. The next day, as his mother was coming out of Viraj's room, he presented her with the glass of water balanced on a silver tray he had stolen from the kitchen. He told her that if she ever had a headache, the rainbow water would make her better.

'How did you know I had a headache?' she asked. And he copied those other words he'd heard daily in Aramani: 'I just had that thought…'

She thanked him and drank down the water in one gulp then squeezed his hand. He hoped this meant she might take him on an outing: a boat-ride on Yanna Lake or a picnic on Jagar Rock. Instead, she announced that she was going to lie down.

'Why is everyone always asleep?' he asked, hitting a nerve in a woman who never managed more than four hours a night. Whereas, when his head touched the pillow he was asleep for ten hours straight, only waking when his mother opened the shutters, filled the bucket for his bath and told him to hurry or he'd miss breakfast.

What Kasper didn't know then was how many hours she'd been up for or how hard she had worked to pacify her mind. His dreams were full of sunlight and monkeys, chapattis and soft faces, so that when he was dressed in clean kurtas, he looked like something newly born.

The muslin veil that hung from Gayan's door had the texture of a cloud. And for the fact of its delicacy and his mother's obsession with cleanliness, it was only when

Kasper was washed and dressed in fresh kurtas that she allowed him to see Gayan.

When he arrived, Kasper would wrap the veil around himself, both to feel the freedom of the sky and to pretend he was his mother dressed in a sari.

'Kasper,' Gayan said one day. 'Stop all that, just be as you are and come here.'

He extricated himself slowly in a performance of dance and disguise. Gayan fished out the finger puppet of a monkey from his desk drawer. Mouth closed, he talked to the monkey as if Kasper were also a monkey, then asked him how many trees he'd swung from that day.

At the moment he stopped speaking, there was the sound of scampering on the roof.

'Listen!' said Gayan.

Outside, a real monkey crouched in twitchy stillness, half a banana between its hands. Kasper watched for a while, thinking how magical Aramani was, for it so often happened that you were talking about something and then it appeared.

'Mama's clever, isn't she?'

'She's one of our best overseas students. And you'll be the same.'

'We didn't come here by sea.'

Gayan smiled, opened another desk drawer and placed a square of brittle biscuit against the boy's lips.

'What's wrong with onions?' Kasper asked as he ate.

'Why worry about onions?'

'I saw one in the market.'

'Well, pay it no attention.'

'Will it come alive?'

Gayan smiled.

'And what's in there?' Kasper pointed to a silver jug.

'Mahua flowers.'

'I can't see any flowers.'

Gayan's hands gestured as if to say that if he didn't see flowers that was his own problem.

'If I die will I become a monkey?

'Too many questions.'

7

Sometimes, Kasper tried a whole day of his mother's routine. He would hear the opening notes of the early morning song that rang out across the campus to wake the residents, see the outline of her body as it swung out of bed, then watch as she tiptoed in the grey light to the bathroom.

Back in the bedroom, she would put on her sari, flick the end up over one shoulder, pinning it to keep it in place. Once dressed, a folded woollen shawl under her arm, she was gone.

In seconds he was behind her. Some days, she sat on the roof; others, she braved the big hall or else she meditated at the base of a stone column that stood at one corner of the courtyard. He decided on the reason for each choice. If on the roof she was worrying about his father. If by the stone column she was feeling weak. When she followed everyone else to the meditation hall it meant she was happy. Wherever she was he sat a little behind and copied her.

But it was Viraj his mother spent most of her time with. As his secretary, she worked in his room overlooking the courtyard. Bored of his own company, Kasper would sit on the balcony and listen to her typing. He didn't know

Hindi well enough to understand what Viraj was dictating; he only went by the cadence of their voices – sometimes soft, as if a prayer were being spoken or a lullaby sung; other times mechanical, full of coughs and the banging of papers on a desk.

At the end of the day, Kasper would lean against the wall outside Viraj's room. For it seemed to him that following his mother around was the only way to keep her close.

One day, small and clean, skin glowing with sleep, his mother told him that Aramani had visitors and he was to be included in a parade of the highest-achieving residents, beginning with the tallest and ending with him – the smallest. Kasper said he didn't want to be the smallest. Nor was he interested in parades and why did you have to be tall to be good? Anyway, he wanted to sit on the swing and draw. She snapped that he couldn't always do what he wanted and that today he had to do as she said, which was to 'sit right here and eat'. She held out a plate of mango slices, and sweets that tasted like tiny treacle puddings.

Full and so placid, he was led to a room he had never seen before. Row upon row of costumes hung from brass rails. Gold, green, turquoise; silks, soft chiffon, taffeta...

'Look!' she cried in a surprising moment of pleasure as she pressed a turban on his head. 'You'll have to wear it until after lunch when the visitors arrive, and then you have to sit on a throne like a prince.'

'Why?'

'Because you are a prince.'

'I'm not.'

'Just for once, Kasper, you have to do what I say. You are a prince; you're very important. And I haven't time to explain.'

By now Kasper was bored. 'Have, have, have to,' he chanted then sneezed.

'Kasper!'

'You like points, Mama! Here's a good point. If I'm sitting on a throne, how will they know I'm the smallest?'

'It's only for a show. Stop asking so many questions. And don't call me Mama. I'm not your mama here.'

'Why not? Anyway I don't want to be in a show. You're always telling me not to show off. I want to draw and then go to the village. *Mama!*'

'Being in Aramani isn't always about what you want. We're given everything here for nothing, so sometimes we have to give something back.'

'Have, have, *have to!*'

Oh, it was all wrong! What he loved about Aramani was the feeling that you could do what you liked, that you didn't need to be part of a display in order to be loved. He longed for the donkey in the marketplace and the cows who congregated around the water pump. So he did what the students of Aramani were always being warned against: took the law into his own hands. And, once free of his mother, who now said she wasn't his mother, he threw off his shoes, rolled up the costume pantaloons, shins stick-thin and bare, and ran to the back gate.

The village children laughed when they saw him. Ignoring them, he moved in great high-kneed strides towards the steps leading to the road that dipped down into the village.

Drawn always to colour, he hung around a store that sold glass bangles, wanting to see how many he could fit on his arm if he kept it outstretched. He chose gold, orange, blue, green, pink, bunching up his fingers to fit the bangles over his knuckles to make the same pattern over and over, until his arm looked like a multi-coloured curtain rail.

'Look! Gold, orange, blue, green, pink, gold, orange, blue, green, pink…'

'Yes. Now take them off.' The bangle-seller's voice was firm.

Agitated, Kasper pulled too hard, and suddenly they were all on the ground, smashed into a game of Pick Up Sticks.

'That will be five thousand rupees.'

'I don't have any rupees.'

'Why do you come to the village with no rupees?' The anger in the bangle-seller's voice made Kasper's face hot. To avoid further reprimand he bent down and scrabbled around on the ground attempting to retrieve every piece of bangle he had broken. Several, he dropped into the deep pocket of his pantaloons.

'I was teasing. They're only worth five hundred. I'll find a way for you to repay me.' And the heat and the fear were suddenly diffused, the bangle-seller biffing his turban so that it sat at an angle on his head.

Wanting to be free, Kasper ran down the hill to the donkey where he hit out at the flies, telling them to stop bothering its eyes. His hand went to his pocket and he retrieved a green stick of glass. 'A bogey!' he shouted and edged it up into the dark recess of the donkey's left nostril.

'There, there, there!' he chanted again, wanting to hear his friend whinnying in open-mouthed objection, to see its gums and tongue and watch it poo. The glass sticks that were left, he arranged in a wigwam at the roots of the fig tree that stood just behind the village bank. From there, he darted away again, this time to the market where he stole an onion.

His mother was facing the bathroom door when he returned to their room.

'Go and wash. Right now! And this time use the scrubbing brush.'

'But I've had two baths today already. It would be a waste of five thousand rupees to have another one.' His mother took no notice, ripped off his clothes, leaving only the turban and told him to move, 'or we'll be late.' Meanwhile, she straightened out his costume and sprayed it with some kind of scent.

Seated as instructed at the end of the row, Kasper sneezed loudly.

'Stop it!' shouted Kala.

'You're not meant to shout.'

'I'm not shouting. I'm telling you not to sneeze or if you do, to do it quietly. You're meant to be giving a vision of peace.'

At this reprimand, a succession of six more sneezes shot from Kasper's nose like bullets. The brothers seated on either side of him laughed, while Kala gave his hand a sharp slap. Furious tears filled his eyes. He was tired and humiliated and in the midst of the laughter he uttered one of the most important lines he was ever to speak as a child.

'I don't understand why I'm here.'

Then he spotted Amba bent over his camera, hair ruffled, teeth pressed down on his bottom lip in concentration. Kasper waved and a light flashed.

'He's your friend?' asked the brother beside him.

'My best friend.'

'Be careful not to love anyone too much.'

This was too adult an instruction for a small boy, and it drove him into his shell. After a while, the inside of his head started itching, as if insects were running about just beneath the surface of his skin.

8

The next day, Amba took him for a ride on his scooter. They drove to Jagar Rock, white clothes reddening with dust, as they crossed into the scrubland away from the main road. Kasper had his arms around Amba's waist, his head against his back, and for stretches of the journey he kept his eyes closed, imagining they were flying across ravines, over treetops and up into the sky, instead of navigating the humps and dips of the heat-dried track.

After Jagar, they had no destination in mind. An hour or so passed before Amba swerved to the side of the road and brought the scooter to a skid-halt. Then he opened the little box on the back of the bike and took out a blanket and a bag of biscuits and sweets.

Together they lay against a rock, eating and staring up at the sky. It was an afternoon of pure joy. Everything was right. He was with the right person, his clothes were dirty, his mouth full of sweets, his mind at peace.

'If I was in London I'd be at school now. It would be raining and I'd be in a classroom with a man shouting.'

Amba leant on one elbow, stroked Kasper's cheek and told him again that he shouldn't underestimate the importance of education.

'But I can learn everything here. With you.'

Amba lay back down and began telling a story about a group of blind people who were taken to visit an elephant.

'That's stupid.'

'No, listen. If you want me to be your teacher, you've got to listen about the elephant. One after the other they were led up to the elephant and asked to say what they thought they were touching. One fellow said it was a tree trunk. Another said it was a leaf, another a ridged piece of wood that was drying in the sun.'

'I told you it was stupid. Why didn't they just say it was an elephant?'

'Exactly. Why didn't they?'

'I don't know,' said Kasper, who had no patience with stories because in Aramani they always ended with a moral, while what he wanted was food and sky and the feeling of Amba beside him.

'The people they asked were blind, Kasper, so they could only describe the elephant according to the part of its body they touched. The fellow who touched the elephant's leg thought it was a tree trunk, the one who touched its ear thought it a leaf and so on and so forth. It's an excellent story. I tell it to myself when there's an argument brewing; that everyone sees things differently.'

'But you said they couldn't see.'

Kasper was annoyed. He had a tummy ache and Amba talked too much. For a while, a melancholy fell upon them and the conversation ended. Then suddenly Amba sat up.

'Look!'

'What?'

Amba swivelled Kasper's head round.

'Can't you see it? A tiger!'

'It can't be.'

'It is. Shh now!'

And they lay on their fronts, hearts pumping against the warm ground until Kasper decided his friend must have been imagining things.

That evening they stayed out after dark, missing the evening meditation, as well as supper. Kasper didn't care, but someone else did. Not his mother, who never seemed to be around, but Kala – the fatso sneeze-hater in whose presence they were both nervous.

'Where have you been? What for? It's far too late to be outside Aramani. Look what you've done to your clothes. No one else goes out like you do. Go and have a bath.' On and on as if they were children. Amba was quiet but Kasper butted in. 'You're breaking a rule getting cross,' and then sneezed three times, to which she responded that it was time he went to bed *at once*.

As they walked off, Kasper asked his friend why he put up with it. Amba brushed the question off, saying it wasn't important, that she was always like that. With the remnants of some hazy schoolboy knowledge of monarchs and battles, Kasper felt this was the wrong answer.

'That's how wars begin, Amba, when people don't fight back. Why don't you hit her?'

Amba laughed, as if Kasper's impudence had relaxed him. Then he suggested food. For these were the days when eating made everything better and, while mealtimes were fixed, as a child, Kasper could always get his hands on food. And if he could, then Amba would too.

That night Kasper felt sick. Sunstroke made him dizzy, and the tiger moved through his mind like danger. When finally he slept, he felt himself being pushed up and

36

out of his own skull as if he were flying. But not in the way Gayan taught, nor as he had pretended he was doing when he was on the back of Amba's scooter. Instead, he was moving above his own body and yet he felt as heavy as stone.

Then he was back in his classroom in London. His form master was wearing a pinstripe suit; Kasper was in his white kurtas, explaining to the class that it was quite normal for people to come to school in the same clothes they slept in; that people in pyjamas could think better than when they were dressed in blazers and trousers. At this, the teacher, a man who looked a little like Viraj, only taller, had opened his desk drawer and started throwing parcels into the air. When the boys opened them to find clean kurtas inside, they scrambled to get undressed, throwing their clothes high into the air. In seconds they were all in white and Kasper was at the front of the class, not in his kurtas but in his mother's sari, telling them they were blind and so they could only see part of a tiger. They listened with interest until the teacher, who was also in pyjamas, clapped loudly. And suddenly they were back in their uniforms.

The dream over, Kasper bumped back into his body, head boiling, mouth dry. His mother's bed was empty. He looked at the tightly tucked sheets and they told him that she wasn't the mother she should be. There was no substance to her, no feeling of her hands on his body, even of her having a body at all. At the same time, he knew she was what men called beautiful, and that made him proud.

That day, it was Kasper's turn to go to the dhobi and fetch the Elders' laundry. After breakfast, he stumbled for a second time into the village. The dhobi tried to give him a boiled sweet but he said he'd had enough sweets.

'Well, what about water, that's what you need?' Kasper took the cup offered and gulped it down fast, only remembering afterwards that it was against the rules to accept refreshment of any kind, even water, from outside Aramani.

'I've put the clothes in piles according to each one's name, so you don't have to sort them out,' said the dhobi. Kasper thanked him, took the washing and placed it in two large canvas bags which dangled from his arms as he walked. He wanted to see the donkey again and check on the little glass wigwam he had constructed out of the broken bangles. But both would mean a detour and the laundry was heavy, so he stomped back up the hill and into the camp, where the children were crying and hitting each other in the heat.

In the courtyard he dumped the bags on the ground and, crouching down, began to sort out which clothes belonged to whom. Usually he enjoyed this task, the carefully made creases satisfying a mind that was slowly beginning to tighten. That day, the clothes weren't arranged in the way the dhobi had said. Trouser legs were wrapped around the arm of a shirt and undergarments hid between the folds of the sisters' saris. Kala's huge knickers he held up in the air and waved like a flag. They were among a pile of her clothes, all of them huge. When he came to his mother's, they seemed mixed in with everyone else's so that her sari was folded between the two legs of a pair of kurta bottoms belonging to a brother.

He stared at her nametape, recognising her own hand. Yasmin. To make it more real he said it out loud: 'Yasmin. Yasmin, Yasmin,' and again, 'Yasmin, Yasmin, Yasmin,' until the sound of the word made him think of some slim animal with sharp teeth and a snout.

Then suddenly he was on a bed.

'You fainted, Kasper. You're safe here.'

In the lap of these words and the fragrance of the room, he fell asleep. When he woke he saw he was in the infirmary that was situated to one side of a narrow alley leading to the kitchens. Large bird-like figures with wide wings hovered above him cooing about buttermilk and rest.

'He's growing fast…'

'More iron in his diet…'

'The heat.'

9

There were times during those early years when Kasper longed to break all that was beautiful about Aramani. When his mother was nowhere to be found and he couldn't get what he was drawing to look right on the page, he would bang his head over and over against the bedroom wall and cry. One day, the residents, in their flat calmness seeming barely to exist, and he longing for the wild leap of a monkey or the prowl of a tiger against which to pit his wits, he snapped five of his best pencils in half.

That same afternoon, he stood at the door of the smallest meditation room and waited while the white sheet was lifted, the floor swept and washed. Then he slipped in and hid behind the life-sized picture of Gayan that stood against the north wall. He was aware that what he was about to do was not just against the rules, it was dangerous. But the urge to destroy was stronger.

At six-thirty the room began to fill. When there were enough residents wrapped in their shawls, heads covered against the evening chill, he shut his eyes, counted to ten and rammed his fist through the picture of Gayan which, lit from behind, illuminated the room. His knuckle burst through the ball of the old man's eye. There was a bang then darkness. The room gasped. On the floor lay the onion he'd stolen from the village. In the time it took for someone to bring a torch, Kasper made a run for it, scarpering into the courtyard and out of the gates down to Yanna Lake where he crouched on the bank.

But someone had seen him as someone saw everything in Aramani, whether it were a sin of the mind or the hand. The next morning, he was hauled up before Anouka and told it was time he had a formal occupation. He must take four baths a day as the grown-up residents did, and work in the vegetable hall.

'From after breakfast until lunchtime.'

Her eyes were on his body, which was no longer as small as it had been. He was twelve and growing too tall to lie in the afternoon with Banhi in her fruit store or to spend time with Amba in his darkroom, indeed any other adult, apart from his mother who seemed, by this time, to have slimmed to the size of a child.

He hated the new routine. The vegetable hall was dark and the brothers who worked there off-hand and brisk. As for that other rule about washing, one night, instead of counting sheep, he counted buckets. Three thousand, three hundred and thirty baths he decided he'd suffered since being in Aramani.

Late morning. Everyone tired of cutting and scraping. Kasper, seated on a rush stool, thinking about the bangle-seller and which colour he might steal from him next, when Raj, a teenage resident with strong muscles and good looks, began singing a Hindi love song. The brother beside him nudged him to be quiet. He took no notice, instead stretching across his admonisher to give Kasper a poke in the arm.

'Why are you here?'

'I'm peeling a potato. Same as you.'

'You're not the same as me. And I don't mean here. I mean in Aramani. Why aren't you in England at school? You're not Indian.'

'Yes I am. Gayan told me I was just as Indian as everyone else.'

'Well he's wrong.'

'Raj!'

'No, don't stop him. I *want* to know what he means.'

'What about your mother? She's not Indian. She shouldn't live here. Foreigners only come here in the winter.'

Kasper waited for someone to come to his rescue.

'Mama works hard here. She works every day for Viraj. She's just as Indian as Viraj.'

'Viraj!'

'Yes. What about Viraj? And what about Mama? She works harder than you. And if I should be in school what about you?'

He hadn't intended those words, didn't even know quite what he meant by them, but was livid at hearing his mother attacked, and for the first time since their arrival, was confused about who he really was.

'And what about Daddy? Where's your *Daddy*?'

'My father's in London.'

'Don't you miss him? Or your *Mama*? Doesn't she miss him? Does he observe the rule of celibacy? Does your *Mama*?'

At this, someone elbowed Raj so hard that his stool tipped sideways and he fell on his backside. There was a

42

half-hearted titter as he staggered to his feet, this huge boy with his paunch and rude health, pointing to the plate on Kasper's lap.

'You don't even cut vegetables properly!' And back on his stool, he held out a handful of carrots that looked like the small houses from a Monopoly board. 'This is how you're meant to do it.'

Kasper had no answer. If he'd been quicker, there were all kinds of retorts he might have made: Raj had spent his whole life cutting carrots; if he couldn't do it right by now, he must be stupid. Anyway, who cared what shape a carrot was cut in? The words found no expression except through his feet. He stood up, pushed away his own stool and kicked Raj hard on the shin.

'Kasper, stop!'

But he kept going, his head splitting with fury, until someone took hold of his arms and restrained him. Then Raj slapped him hard on the cheek. And suddenly, as if summoned by the sound, there was Gayan, standing in the doorway.

The scene fell apart. The brothers resumed their seats but Kasper could sit no longer. He didn't want to see Gayan either. So he ran to the only place, other than Amba's darkroom and Banhi's fruit store, where he felt comfortable: the milk kitchen.

The twin brothers who worked in the milk kitchen were large and soft, as if made of the milk they served up. They had beautiful singing voices, which counteracted the narrow whine of the music that was piped through the tannoy system once every few hours to call the

43

residents into silence. When the twins sang the same tunes, they made them into tender, rounded harmonies, opening their mouths wide as if unafraid to live a life that brought pleasure.

They worked in a small room at the back of the main cooking area, one stirring the milk with a stick that looked like a rounders bat, the other tidying and stocking the spice shelves. The fact that you could barely tell the difference between them seemed to Kasper a miracle, created not in the womb of a mother but by the magic of Aramani herself.

When Kasper arrived that lunchtime, they were seated in canvas chairs like a middle-aged couple on a beach, one beating out the rhythm to a new song, the other crooning the lyrics. Urgent to confess as much as to be forgiven, Kasper butted in uninvited.

'I hit Raj!'

Consumed by the elusiveness of the tune, they simply nodded and went on. Kasper envied their indifference, sensing that such simplicity was either the answer to life or the death of it. Still, they managed to distract him, telling him to sing the sound 'ahhh' over and over on one note. He thought of London where a doctor had once asked him to open his mouth so he could examine his tonsils. And the connection felt like a solution.

Soon he had a cup of hot milk laced with cardamom and ginger in his hands and, seated on the chair they always kept for him, he began to feel better. But because they hadn't given him the chance to speak of what troubled him, when he left he was back with the unresolved guilt of his offence.

In the evenings, residents took it in turns to stir the milk. Kasper enjoyed watching everyone line up for tea, as if they too needed a dose of attention. Some liked their tea black, others with hot milk. Those with stomach problems asked for extra ginger. Whatever spice they favoured, it was Kasper who climbed up to fetch it.

Once, when he was bored and so wanted to be told off, he snuck into the milk kitchen before the twins arrived. The huge vats reminded him of snails and tortoises and England. In search of an equivalent shell, he climbed into one of them, then out again and into another where he knelt curled, enjoying the silver cold of the steel through his white clothing.

When the twins appeared, he jumped up and pointed a pretend gun – 'Boom, boom, boom! You're dead!' Instead of telling him off, they clattered with laughter, although he was made to scrub the pot afterwards.

Those were the days of freedom when the world might have revolved around the sun or the sun the earth. And when Kasper looked up at the stars, he imagined each was another planet where someone identical had just hidden in a steel vat and was now drinking cinnamon milk. Anything was possible in the milk kitchen and yet something was missing from it too.

10

After the incident with Raj, Kasper began to change. No longer did he walk freely into Anouka's room, knowing by instinct that she loved him less now that he was as tall as a young tree. When he visited Banhi in the fruit store he teased her; Amba, he nagged constantly to take him for rides on his scooter.

Once, he decided to take a trip on a bus because he wanted to see what the boats on Yanna Lake looked like from high up; he was curious, too, to know how far from Aramani he could travel without anyone noticing his absence. When a fellow passenger spotted him crouched behind a seat, the bus driver called out his name and told him to come and sit beside him, then threatened to report him to Gayan. Kasper snapped that it would be he who did the reporting.

'I'll say that you kidnapped me.'

'It's not me who's kidnapped you,' said the driver.

Perhaps seeing the fear on Kasper's face, the driver offered him a cigarette and a betel nut to chew and drove him round the lake and into the village. But, after all that, Kasper found a ride wasn't what he wanted; the boats looked no different, the driver smelt of garlic and he hated the cigarette when he smoked it.

His mother was tight with fury when she found out.

'Aramani is heaven on earth. And that driver is from hell. You shouldn't even have talked to him. Now you'll have to have another bath and iron your own kurtas. It's too late to send anything to the dhobi.'

The only iron in the building where they slept received the full force of his fury. He waited and waited but the electricity that day was faulty, and with only a table for an ironing board, it was hard to make any impact on his clothes. Banging the iron up and down, Kasper made a burn in the shape of a boat on his kurta trousers.

'You can't wear those,' said his mother. 'You'll have to go to bed until the afternoon.' And he stood before her, swiping his arm through the air as if knocking down a line of skittles that he imagined were a group of brothers standing in a row.

That evening, when he was in bed making a giant-sized drawing of a betel nut, his mother came and sat on his bed. Her voice was soft.

'Kasper, I've been unkind. I'm sorry. It's Surya. He isn't well. I have to go back to London. I've arranged for you to travel as far as Delhi with me, but then you must return to Aramani. I won't be more than a few months. Everyone here will look after you.'

The statements were so simple that Kasper continued with his drawing but his bare legs felt like twigs as he slid them up and down against the sheet.

'When are you going?'

'Tomorrow.'

Perhaps it was the one-word answer that marked

the beginning of the gradual process of hardening that happened in his soul. He had always liked surprises, but not this kind of surprise, for he could barely remember his father's name, let alone picture him or what he meant. In the end, not able to conjure any real feeling, he manufactured one, which was to jump at the prospect of having the bedroom to himself and a rest from his mother's constant nagging: baths, clean clothes, silence, and the million other things that seemed to have turned her into a tight stick of a person to whom he no longer belonged. Nor was he bothered when she told him to be careful of Kala. Kasper retorted that he was always careful of Kala, he knew what she was like.

'She sees us as outsiders, Kasper.'

The word outsider triggered a genuine feeling. For, whatever his behaviour, Kasper had come to feel through and through that Aramani was his home.

'And watch out for Raj.'

Kasper worked hard at the betel nut as the mention of Raj's name caused a rush of emotion: guilt that he hadn't told his mother about hitting him; confusion over whether, in that case, he really loved her; anger with Raj; and then with his mother again for implying that he wasn't strong enough to face adversity. It was the paper on which he drew that suffered the force of his feelings. He suddenly ripped it from his sketchpad and hurled it across the room. It landed on the chair where his clothes for travelling were folded ready.

'You'll have to wash them again.'

'WHAT?'

'I was teasing.'

It was the first time in years she had been light-hearted

with him. Perhaps she was glad to be going? Perhaps she didn't like it here after all?

The next morning, Kasper sat in the courtyard, waiting, in the way one was always waiting in Aramani: for lunch to begin, meditations to finish, classes to end, vegetable cutting to be over. But those were familiar waits. Already sensitive to the quality of the space between one scene and the next, this delay felt bumpy for there being nothing known or understood at the end of it.

When she finally appeared, he was seated ready and cross-legged on the ground just inside the front gates, his back against their luggage. His mother was running from one door to another, as if involved in a series of farewells, her last to Viraj, whose workroom overlooked the courtyard. His body pelted up behind her. He wanted to listen, aware even then of a closeness between them that he didn't understand. A wave of anxiety moved through him as he heard her cry.

Back in the courtyard, he asked if she had said goodbye to Gayan. 'Of course. I went yesterday. I knew he'd be busy this morning.'

'But he loves you. He says you're his best *overseas* student.'

'That's nonsense!'

Kasper felt hurt at this dismissal of praise when all he was trying to do was console her.

No Elders were there at the moment of their departure. This, too, distressed him. Usually when a resident set out on a journey, members of the community gathered to say goodbye. That morning, only Banhi turned up, bringing with her a bag of fruit. 'For you to eat on the train.'

His mother hugged her tight and whispered something in her ear. Who knows what had passed between them?

And now it was too late to ask.

11

The journey to Delhi was the first Kasper had taken for five years. As they sat waiting for the train, he was struck by the contrast between the brightly coloured station stalls selling snacks, magazines and plastic toys, and the clean, high air of his Aramani home.

The train itself made him edgy. Although they were in a first-class carriage, they shared it with a family who sprawled across the seats and talked late into the evening.

His mother sat by the window, curled under a blanket. By the time they arrived, she looked even smaller than she had in Aramani. He kept telling himself there was nothing to worry about, that it was only a train journey offering a new view of India, but he didn't believe himself.

The trouble eased when the train drew into New Delhi, where they were greeted by a group of women dressed like the sisters in Aramani who transported them to a house where they were to stay for the night. But the worry returned in the morning when his mother sat beside him on her bed and handed him a piece of paper with his father's address and phone number on it.

'Keep this safe, Kasper.'

Staring at the paper, he waited while his mother disappeared into the bathroom. In a reversal of their first day in Aramani, when she had suddenly transformed herself from young mother to sister, now she emerged from the bathroom dressed in jeans and a blue top, her hair free of its plait. He stared at the blonde down on her forearms, noticing for the first time the long, slim delicacy of her fingers. Seeing her in this new form provoked in him a brief but powerful longing for the life of his past: to go with her to London; meet his old school friends; sit in a café; eat a hamburger...

'You've got to go back to Aramani, Kasper. I'll see you soon.'

'Will you? I can't find you now and you're still here.'

'I'm with you, Kasper.'

'You're not.'

'I'm only going for a few months.'

'No, you're abandoning me,' he said, although in truth he felt nothing.

Perhaps the veil that Aramani drew over all difficult emotions had stretched down the mountain, across the plains and all the way to Delhi. And perhaps that was a blessing because he never saw again this woman who had both protected and ignored him.

12

On the twelve-hour train journey back to Aramani, ruthless and blank, Kasper decided it was time to leave aside all that was natural about life. He would no longer be a boy growing gradually into adolescence, but a brother committed to The Philosophy.

As the train moved slowly across the wide plains of Jaipur, he stared at the paper on which his mother had written his father's address, deciphering and learning by heart the small rounded letters, folding it up and hiding it in the flap of his notebook. Then he jotted down in single words and pictures a list of things he would do differently on his return to Aramani: attend early morning meditations; not go back to bed afterwards but follow them with a bath and the first class of the morning; stop talking to Amba about scooters and cricket; avoid all physical fights; and ration his visits to the milk kitchen to three times a week.

When the list was complete he drew a cricket bat. Soon, the other passengers decided it was night and he climbed up to the top bunk to sleep. His dreams tried to serve him, presenting him with images of cinnamon milk and cricket runs. He woke crying, then became furious with his tears. How could a grown-up intent on devotion succumb to such weakness? He had discovered already the danger of tears, how they made holes in your mind, left you empty and open to invasion. He had no mercy on himself and, as a punishment, decided he wouldn't eat the food the sisters in Delhi had given him.

This effort of will lasted until Ajmer, when a family in the same carriage laid out their breakfast on the seat beside him. Out came the package and in seconds he had eaten the whole of a sweet roti and a bag of squashed chips.

In the early afternoon, he arrived back in Aramani, grubby and muddled, the stink of the train in his nostrils.

A good night's sleep restored his resolve and he marched to Anouka's room to tell her his plan. She appeared not to have heard and simply stared at him as if assessing the ripeness of a piece of fruit. Then she picked up the phone to summon Amba. Within minutes, Kasper's old friend was standing in the doorway, teeth jammed down on his lower lip.

'I want you to explain The Philosophy to Kasper. From the beginning.'

'Why from the beginning?'

'Everyone has to start from the beginning.' And she waved them both away.

'Does she want to get rid of us?'

Amba looked down. 'I don't think so. She's just busy. If you want proper lessons, Kasper, you'll have to behave. We'll start next Monday.'

Kasper looked blank.

'The day they serve sweet rotis with tea.'

Now a smile, for he was relieved to be back in a place

where, for so long, he had marked the days of the week not by name but by what he associated with them.

In the weeks that followed he and Amba spent Monday afternoons in the little teaching room situated on the south side of the courtyard. As a teacher Amba was not the person Kasper knew and loved. He was troubled in some way, as if he found what he explained difficult to live by yet had accepted it so deeply that speaking of it no longer involved thought.

'As Anouka instructed, we will start from the beginning and move by the linear method.'

The beginning was the soul. Kasper told him he knew the beginning was the soul, he didn't want the beginning, he wanted the end. Amba took no notice, explaining parrot-fashion what Kasper had learnt aged seven, that the body was a car, the soul its driver and that without the soul, the car could go nowhere.

'I know all that. It's boring. I want to know where the planets are and how to fly.'

'Don't be stupid. That's not why you're here.'

'But I've heard everything you're saying before. I want something new.'

'There's nothing new. You don't need anything new. Remember the slogan *old is gold*.'

'*Be free to see, think and you sink, old is gold*. It's all stupid.'

'It's not stupid. Old things are the most valuable. Repeated things are valuable, too. So you do need to go from the beginning. And the beginning is that the soul is like a bird that flies. When you are silent your soul flies like a bird.'

'But that means birds ride in cars. That's stupid.'

'You know exactly what I am saying and why I'm saying it. Your body, a car; your soul, a bird.'

In search of a more vivid connection, Kasper retorted again that it would surely be interesting to start at the end of The Philosophy and finish with the beginning.

At this Amba laughed and Kasper looked down on him for allowing himself to be knocked off his pedestal by a child. He was filled with shame by his next move, which was to seek out Anouka and tell her he wanted Viraj not Amba to teach him; Viraj was more serious.

Anouka snapped that The Philosophy was the same whoever taught it. He quoted back a line he had heard in a class that knowledge spoken without power is empty. Then he told her that that's what he felt when Amba was teaching – it was empty. He prickled with discomfort at this insult to his old friend and was relieved when she turned down his request by raising her enormous hand in a dismissive NO.

13

In the second lesson Kasper was silent as Amba explained Aramani's concept of God; how Gayan's body transported not just his own soul, but God's soul too, The Philosophy conveyed from one to the other in a sort of whisper inside the old man's head. Again, like a person who regards a diamond merely as a combination of carbon and pressure, Kasper was indifferent, while for most this was the insight that explained what made Aramani so strange, and why everyone who visited said there must be more to the place than the humans who lived in it.

Amba ended their second lesson with five minutes of silence. Not the kind of silence you could relax in, but one in which you were under exactly that pressure, forced to keep your eyes open and stare.

As a child, when the residents stared at each other, Kasper had simply looked down. Later, he mastered a squint so that he was looking in the right direction but everything was pleasantly blurred. With Amba he knew he could no longer fall back on this trick. Besides, after his visit to Anouka he wanted to punish himself, to concentrate so hard that he could feel the full impact of his betrayal.

The meditation began and with difficulty Kasper kept

his eyes open. Looking at Amba, transfixed as always by the way his friend's upper lip stretched down like a camel's over his top teeth, his mind reared up in rebellion.

After three or so very long minutes, boredom gave way to curiosity for Amba's face suddenly began to glow like a Halloween pumpkin. This image led him to London and his mother, and then his mind lost its way. But the silence went on, and the light brightened and brightened until he had to cover his eyes. Through splayed fingers it came to him in stripes, more and more piercing, and only in white. And the white wasn't sunlight but a force with a presence.

'What was that?'

'What was what?'

'Didn't you see it? That light?'

'No more than usual.'

'But it was blinding.'

'It must have been for you, Kasper. My body's aching all over. It's a good thing you saw it. It will help you.'

To their third lesson, Amba arrived late, a smear of oil down one cheek.

'You should take a bath.'

There was a tightness to Amba's laugh. 'No, no, it was the scooter. It broke down. I had to push it all the way back from the village.'

'Have you mended it now?'

'No. It's kaput.'

Kasper felt sorry for his friend and noticed he wasn't as clear in his teaching that day. Towards the end of the lesson, Amba leant forward conspiratorially. 'I'm going to tell you a secret, Kasper. It's about the scooter we ride on. I stole it. It was outside the bank for a year. I checked it three or four times over the months to make sure it didn't belong to any of the fellows who work there. Then one day I told myself that if it hadn't been used all that time it couldn't be much good to anyone so I'd steal it and do it up. It took me five months. That was a year ago. And now it's conked out completely.'

'Is that the secret?'

'Yes. That I stole it. But the secret behind the secret is that it's broken because I stole it.'

'I don't see why,' Kasper said, thinking of how many hundreds of bangles he had taken without punishment since being in Aramani. 'If it was old, it would have broken anyway, and you don't know that it broke because you stole it. That was a year ago. The punisher would have forgotten after a whole year.'

'Maybe, maybe not. It was working when I rode it up the mountain. And you'll see again and again that this is the way life works. Break a rule and it breaks you back. And that, my friend, is the law of karma.'

Despite his resolution to commit himself fully to The Philosophy, Kasper found this lesson worrying. For so long he had ranged about Aramani freely, been loved, spoilt even. Now he was being shown the rules of the place, the silent judgement that hovered just beneath its surface. And Amba was right – sometimes the judge came up to bite.

A dream. One that belonged to his adolescent body and the future it yearned for.

59

He was lying on Jagar Rock with a man. Nothing was clear other than the warmth and the touch, the feel of strong arms around his shoulders, and together they were enacting a movement of which his mind knew nothing. Yet they were doing it thoroughly and beautifully in the naked air. He woke to wet sheets and shame.

In an effort to absolve himself he scrubbed his body hard with a plastic brush. Then attended the morning class. As the day went on, the dream faded. But the action he'd taken felt like a lump in his throat. So, submitting to the child in himself, he sought Banhi. As usual, she was on her chair in the sunshine. As usual, in silence. She didn't look up, didn't smile or stretch out her hand to hold his. After sitting with him for several minutes she finally disappeared into her fruit store, emerging with a shrivelled orange perched on her palm as if it were something unclean.

'For you.'

Kasper stared at the orange, then at her, and wondered if she could see the sin in his eyes and was punishing him, for usually she gave him the best of the fruit.

That afternoon, as he was resting, Raj and another brother walked into his bedroom, opened his mother's cupboard and removed all her clothing.

'What are you doing?'

'What I've been told to do.'

'What's that?'

'What we're doing now.'

'But her shawl. I want to keep Mama's shawl,' Kasper cried. Raj shook his head, lifted up the bed, carried it onto the balcony, sawed off its legs and removed it. Later, Kasper heard that both mattress and clothes had been burnt.

14

On the stone ledge outside his room, Kasper stood looking up at the mountains and thought once more about the dream, about being given a shrivelled orange, then about Raj barging into his room so vindictively.

If only he could go to Banhi now and ask her what had really happened that day. If she said 'I remember it well. You came in search of comfort because you had sinned in your sleep', he would know what his young self had always believed: that the force of karma which swept daily through Aramani wasn't a figment of his imagination. If, instead, she laughed at him, and asked how could she be expected to know what another person got up to in their sleep, or if she said that the oranges just happened to be small that year, the fact that he had long attributed too much significance to small events would be confirmed.

But what could she tell him – about himself, his mother, anything?

He wondered how she had come to lose her senses in such a short time and, if someone as innocent as Banhi had to suffer, what the law of karma really meant. Perhaps she was paying for someone else's sin? Or perhaps the force that dealt out reward and punishment was random?

Or there was no force?

No law?

And no maker of the law?

Of all the thoughts that troubled him now, this last was the one that frightened him most.

His mind turned to the conditions of his stay:

Eat with the Elders.

Work the lift.

Cause us no trouble.

Dressed in clean kurtas, he left his room and walked down the road towards the teaching block. He was fifteen when it had been built to cater for the growing numbers of visitors keen to be a part of Aramani's version of human history. The lift he had operated in his youth was an affectation, suggesting the organisation was bigger than it was. The building stood five storeys high, but many rooms on the upper floor remained unused. And as a student fresh out of Amba's lessons, Kasper had been determined not to regard the task as menial. Instead, he decided he'd use the role to advertise his spiritual status. To each person who entered he would offer an aspect of his learning.

As he resumed his place on the stool by the door, the memory of such arrogance filled him with shame, not only because of the way he had once mythologised the lift, but also because it was in this small, unglamorous space that he had met the person who was to take from him his life. He tried not to think about it or about who might have operated the lift since his departure. Both thoughts brought confusion. His seducer was a girl; his feelings for her had once bordered on love. As for the lift, it seemed to him now to be the symbol of his total self-deception.

During this first shift of his return, he became caught up with a woman who introduced herself as Mina. Clearly wealthy, and keen to attend every lecture on offer, she was also unwieldy. An oversized bag hung from her shoulder and the bulk of her coloured sari made her body seem lumpy and ill.

'I don't know where I want to go,' was her first line. 'I thought there was a lecture on the third floor but now I think it might be on the fifth floor. Do you know where it is?'

'The fifth floor is up.'

'Yes, yes, but the lecture, where is the lecture?'

'I don't know. I just work the lift. I'm not in charge of lectures.'

'But you're wearing white. You must know.'

At this non-sequitur, Kasper was relieved to find he hadn't entirely lost his sense of humour.

'I don't see why you're smiling. I'm going to be late. Please take me to the ground floor. I'll get out and ask someone where the lecture is and then I'll get in again. Thank you.'

Kasper pressed the button, the lift seemed very slightly to swing as it fell.

She was gone for half an hour. In the meantime, others entered, including a young woman in Western clothes.

'I'm sorry. I'd like the third floor,' she said.

'Why are you sorry?'

'Because it must be boring just sitting there.'

This statement took him aback for being both true and diminishing.

'I'm fine.'

'I'm Alice.'

'This is the third floor.'

Alice alighted, turning back to smile in a way characteristic of those visiting Aramani for the first time. Then there was Mina again, huge in contrast with the light-footed Alice and her smile.

'The lecture is on the fourth floor.'

'The fourth floor it is.'

When the lift stopped she just stood there.

'We're here.'

'Yes but it's already begun. I think I'll go back to my room.'

'Make up your mind,' Kasper's voice was harsh in its address to himself as well as to her: *make up your mind, decide what you believe, want, love, hate, accept, reject...* Over and over he berated himself.

On returning to his room, he found a plate of fresh fruit on the table.

So. Aramani had expelled him. For had he still been a resident, surely the fruit would have been as shrivelled as the punishing orange Banhi had given him after his dream all those years ago. His upset surprised him. Because he hadn't reckoned on wanting to be an insider again either.

15

When it was time for Kasper's next lesson with Amba, his friend rushed in late to the teaching room, announcing that he had got his hands on another run-down scooter. Excitedly, he suggested they ride to the local temple and have their lesson there. In all his new intensity, Kasper thought this a deviation from seriousness. But once seated behind his friend, eyes closed, speeding along the narrow mountain roads, he realised how much he had missed their excursions, which were without any aim save enjoyment and the glimpse of a mountain tiger.

The temple itself he had seen many a time. A tour once with Gayan, another with Puki and Anil, the brothers from the milk kitchen. But on the day of this lesson, as he watched the temple come into view, Kasper felt a different joy – as if life was, just for a moment, exactly as it should be. On the one hand, he was going to learn something special; on the other, he was in the company of the person he most loved.

It was seated side by side on the temple steps that Amba explained one of The Philosophy's most difficult concepts: that of time and how it runs not in a straight line or even a spiral but round and round like the hands of a clock, so that whatever is going on now will one day happen again in exactly the same way.

'Which means Raj will hit me over and over again. And I'll be kicking him forever. What's the point of that?'

'There's no point to it. It just is. And you won't remember the last cycle when you're in the new cycle. It will all feel new. So listen, Kasper. We're going into the temple to look at the statues.

'I've seen the statues loads of times.'

'But what you need to understand is that the statues are representations of what we used to be.'

'We weren't elephants.'

'No, we weren't elephants, but we were like the goddesses in their alcoves.'

'But I'm a boy.'

'You're a boy now, but you'll have been female in many of your births. That's not the point anyway. The point is about how you were once perfect and that's what you're working to become again so that one day you'll be a deity who is worshipped. Then, over time, you'll lose your power and that's why we're here, learning again how to regain our perfection. And one of the ways we learn to be perfect is to free ourselves of all attachments so that we return to the world in possession of the same dignity as the statues we're about to visit.'

'I'm tired.'

'You mean it's too complicated. But it's important, Kasper. Because to make this happen, nobody in Aramani gets married or lives with their families or has children.'

'Where do people come from then? We came from London.'

Amba laughed.

'I mean it, Amba. Raj? Where is he from? And all the

66

other brothers, how did they get here?'

'All right, I'll tell you. I'll tell you about Raj and you'll
see why he is as he is.'

If at this Kasper was all agog he was also anxious.

'Don't tell me.'

'You need to know Kasper. Raj belongs to Kala. He's
Kala's son.'

'But you just said nobody had children and nobody
got married.'

While his body knew better, Aramani was still a
magical place to Kasper – a paradise where all things
floated high and free and distinct. Now Amba was telling
him that two of those free beings were joined; that they
were as they were, not because of Aramani but because of
each other. He was also jealous because, if individuals in
Aramani belonged to each other, he belonged to no one.

He was suddenly flailing under an unexpected grief.
He'd been wrong to tell Anouka that he already knew The
Philosophy. He could see now that, when applied to life
rather than described in a lecture, it contained layer after
layer of contradiction. He would never be able to sort it
all out, to achieve highly, to understand. Everything was
wrong. And if it was wrong now and Amba was right
about time being cyclical, it would be wrong over and
over again.

> *Doubts will come but just when you feel you are lost, I*
> *will always step in.*

But it wasn't Gayan who stepped in. Gayan was
hidden from view, a silent form always in solitude, always
studying. It was Amba who came to his rescue. Despite

67

Kasper's fear of the depth of his feelings, he and Amba were as close as any two people could be in Aramani. And Kasper knew that if he ran away it would be Amba who'd be blamed. So, he got up, slowly climbed the steps that led up to the temple and returned to his friend.

From past visits, Kasper knew it was stone-cool inside; knew, too, how he had always wanted to run from it for it was like standing in a mother-of-pearl shell making the sound of the sea in his ears. To the eyes, it was gaudy. Everywhere, garlands in orange and pink, decorated faces, falsely sculpted fingers curled in positions of dance, feet raised as if to jump. And the smell – too potent. Like a fire smouldering and burnt out. Coolness and heat mixed together and, through it all, the staring of stucco eyes.

But that day, the little gods in their alcoves seemed each more calmly alive, each signalling a different message of reassurance. The pillars, too, were taller than he remembered. Strangest of all were the gilded elephants, which, solid and towering, seemed yet to be suspended in mid-air. As he stared at their huge golden heads, Kasper felt that he, too, was being raised up, his feet floating off the ground.

Turning to Amba for ballast, he saw that his friend's face had changed. This time, it wasn't a trick of the light; his very features were different, so that Kasper was looking at another face imprinted upon his, and the second face wasn't narrow or tired, but young and noble. It was also a face Kasper knew.

The face he had met and loved in his dream.

16

After all the lessons with Amba in which Kasper privately believed he had seen through a hole in time to the past and could travel there at will, a moment came when he put an end to all questions, all emotions, deciding instead he would stand as firm and unshakeable as the pillars in the temple. Such discipline would mean he would no longer be at the mercy of whim; in fact, it would make him Aramani's most distinguished student.

Yet, with each step Kasper took towards spiritual accomplishment, his mother, now in London, was unable to concentrate on anything but the weekly assaults upon her body. While doctors tried their best to sweep her system clean of tumours over which even the most powerful of surgeons had no purchase, her son applied the same ruthless process to the cleansing of his soul.

And so, over the following few years, Aramani allowed him entry into its double life and the childhood home, until then experienced only as a happy mesh of pleasures, gradually closed in on him, finally narrowing into a tight, unforgiving structure whose beauty lay in its severity. People would appear just when he was thinking of them; tests seemed set specifically to challenge his stamina, and at the last minute would come to nothing.

Water ran out, once even food. But never so they starved.

As for Amba, he came to symbolise for Kasper another kind of double life. He still enjoyed rides on his friend's scooter, still loved to rest his head against that dear, strong back and close his eyes as they sped along the mountain paths and took the steep narrow ride up to Guru Shikar, the highest point of the mountain. But he also became competitive. When Amba told him, 'Even now I fail. After Gayan, only Anouka and Viraj have really mastered silence,' Kasper decided he would outdo them all.

Eventually, he began ignoring Amba and followed Viraj instead. Amba was human and warm; Viraj was clinical. Kasper was fascinated by the way he sat so upright in the courtyard after lunch, folded his newspaper once, twice, three times to make a long rectangle. To Kasper, he seemed a perfect work of art, each pose an image he wanted to draw and hold on to for posterity.

In order to copy him, Kasper began rising an hour earlier than everyone else. He would take a sheet from his notebook on which he wrote, still in his child's hand, a thought from The Philosophy, walk to a private spot beneath one of the khejri trees and stare at the words:

Only one thousand souls will ever reach perfection.

With the aim of being not in the first thousand but the first hundred, first fifty even – and when he was at his most confident, the first ten – he would repeat the thought over and over in his head. Relaxed and self-important, he would then lay his mind the full length of the thought until he felt as if he was being rocked back and forth in a hammock. Occasionally the hammock would move with particular force and his thoughts would shift into silence. Coming as gifts to his ego, these nudges towards height were exactly the proof he needed that there was an external force applauding his efforts.

Just as often, when he exerted too much pressure, there was no laying down of his mind and no silence to follow. It was then that he remembered being a child in England and winding up his first watch. Again and again it had stopped, until he had shown it to his father, who had told him it was broken and would have to be replaced.

But you can't replace your mind.

In his pride, Kasper never asked Amba or Viraj why his thoughts fell flat in this way; he wanted to find out for himself.

After a few weeks, the answer came. Viraj was giving a class. And as if the silencing of the mind were as easy as taking a stroll around Yanna Lake, he declared, 'The Philosophy isn't enough for some students. They make up great myths for themselves, compare themselves to others, when all the mind needs are three words: *I am Peace.*'

So for weeks Kasper silently chanted *I am Peace.* Later, he began saying it aloud. 'Hello, Amba – *I am Peace.* That dhal looks good *I am Peace. I am Peace,* do I have to collect the clothes from the dhobi again...?'

'You sound like a parrot,' Banhi snapped one morning as he ate from a bunch of grapes. This hurt. But he knew she was right, for he was young and what his nervous system needed was the feel of another body against his, the adventure of travel, or a set of chemical experiments to challenge him.

It was then that he would return to the milk kitchen and sit with the twins; or to Amba, and they would run down to the village and play cricket, a game he enjoyed for the freedom it gave and there being no punishment if you lost.

17

Three days after resuming his old routine working in the lift, a thought arose in Kasper's mind with such clarity that it brought him to a standstill in the middle of the courtyard:

> *There will be no peace until you talk to the people you love.*

So, having intended to return to his room, he took a right to Banhi's fruit store, a small building secreted in a hedged-off garden in which there was also a two-seated swing. The afternoon heat glared. Banhi's chair was empty. He waited for a minute or so. Then conscious of a dull pain in his back, he dropped to the ground and crouched against the wall.

A sprinkler revolved slowly on the dried-out grass; a servant wandered past and started sweeping the path. Then a young brother he didn't recognise, who ignored him. This riled Kasper. Having been as haughty himself, he was intolerant now.

'Where's Banhi?'

'Banhi?'

'And Amba? Where's Amba?'

A shrug.

'Amba, buck teeth, had a scooter, lived here for years.'

The brother said that as far as he knew no one of that name lived here now.

'But everyone knows Amba.'

'Describe him again.'

'Like I said, buck teeth, often rides a scooter, plays the fool…' The memories hurting, he pressed on. 'If you don't know him, I'd be grateful if you could ask someone. He was my teacher. I'd like to see him again.'

The young man appeared reluctant. Kasper watched him struggle and manipulated him.

'It doesn't matter. You're busy.'

And the response was as his own would have been when he was sixteen and examined his conscience more than ten times a day.

'It does matter. I'll meet you here at two-thirty tomorrow with an answer. But first, who are you?'

'Kasper Chaudhury.'

'That is your body's name only.'

'I'm fully au fait with Aramani's notion of dualism.'

As soon as he'd said dualism, Kasper felt guilty again. He wasn't entirely sure of the word's meaning himself. As for au fait, from where that term had made its way into his brain, or how it might look in writing, he had no idea.

'I'm sorry. I didn't mean that.'

Too late.

'I'll be here with news of your friend at two-thirty tomorrow.'

When two-thirty came, there was no sign of the brother. Instead, there was Amba himself, seated in the shade of a banyan tree. How small he looked compared to the muscular Lars in his tight white T-shirt, who had introduced Kasper to the gym in Amsterdam and also, he must admit it to himself, whom Kasper had loved; as a body, an adult, a guide who knew the world as he never would.

And yet this love too. What was this love he felt for Amba, the friend of his childhood and the beginning of his learning…?

Softly, with the old delicacy of feeling by which he had lived each second as a student in Aramani, Kasper went to sit next to him.

No movement.

No smile.

'Who was that brother who told you I wanted to see you? He said he didn't know you.'

Amba stared at the grass, his lashes almost navy in their darkness. Kasper moved round to face him.

'Amba, I would have told you about leaving. But how? I came here as a child. I loved it, but I didn't choose it. I didn't sign on a dotted line any more than Raj did.'

'We loved you.'

'We?'

'We.'

'But I was a child.'

'Maybe, maybe not.'

'I've got a new scooter. They gave it to me after you left.'

For being, Kasper guessed, the only way Amba had of expressing his love, the words hurt more than any Lars might have spoken.

'I've come back to see you, Amba. To see everyone. But you especially. Since my father died, I've got nobody.'

'Your father?'

'Heart attack.'

'Your father died?'

'On Boxing Day.'

Amba picked at a piece of grass and Kasper noticed his bitten nails for the first time. Then, breaking every rule of The Philosophy, Amba tipped slightly towards him, held Kasper by the shoulders and kissed him.

'Raj works with the boats on Yanna,' he gabbled, pulling away.

'Amba, don't go!'

'I must. I have a lot to do.'

'Thank you.'

'For what?'

Kasper shrugged, unable to voice his gratitude. Amba had done something extraordinary. Not just hugged but kissed him. Chaste. But still a kiss. Which was how all sins were committed in Aramani: fast and in hiding, then absorbed by the air, in the way the crude stink of hing was absorbed by the heat of the flame.

That evening, Kasper lay on his bed and listened to the mountain dogs howl as if sounding out his own sorrow.

Perhaps he had hurt people's feelings but that wasn't his fault. What he had told Amba was true. There was no graceful way of leaving Aramani. It was an organisation, and also a family, and one that didn't allow you to grow up because if you grew up you left. This was a thought he'd had many times: the business of growing up, leaving, returning, of what he would find once back. He remembered the light he had seen in his lesson with

Amba in the temple. Would he ever be able see it again? Or was it as impossible as it was for a person to regain their virginity? One thing he knew: if the light were taken from him for all time, his existence would cease to have any meaning at all.

18

An early summer morning.

Barely need for a shawl to keep off the chill.

Although teased for his manic repetition of words from The Philosophy, Kasper had faithfully persisted with his studies.

In the large classroom with its cloth-covered floor, he positioned himself in the same upright stance as Viraj, started silently on his words, working them into himself as if polishing a shoe. And for no reason he could understand, unless it was Viraj's quiet form in front of him, his mind finally settled. Stillness held his body until he felt as if he were being lifted free of the earth altogether and was floating in a huge space, the air both light and weighted with embrace.

So.

He had made it.

Reached the peak of the mountain, experienced it fully and known that any decision made from here would be the right decision, any thought the right thought.

But then all that was habitual reared its head: what's for breakfast? Why were scooters mentioned in the class yesterday? Is Amba in trouble? Where did I leave my sketchpad?

At such interruptions he was livid. Questions so trivial were like the nagging screeches of a child, reminding him of the noise that he imagined in the space of a few moments had been permanently eradicated. Another of Aramani's tricks. It took you into peace, made you think you were free, when the fact was you had to light fire after fire to burn the debris inside you.

Amba had warned him.

But he hadn't listened.

Again and again, he suffered. Systematically the place brought him down. As the youngest resident, it was he who had to open the boxes of notebooks that arrived for new students; he who collected the laundry from the dhobi, chopped vegetables, occasionally even worked in the kiosk that sold mementos for visitors to take home. Anything to ensure that he talked, took part, spoke of what was ordinary and practical. He kicked off such tasks fast, like shoes that constricted his movement. He was exceptional, a scholar; every rule of the mind should be followed:

Do not think about others.

Banish any desire other than the desire for peace.

Do not indulge in unnecessary conversation.

Do not take extra helpings at mealtimes.

On and on, until he narrowed and narrowed, and his young body grew as tall and slim as his mind. Occasionally, as well as Aramani interrupting, his own mind kicked up and he'd have one of his dreams: naked boys dancing in the courtyard; Kala rolling down a hill in a petticoat; sometimes himself rolling... He also suffered back pain from sitting too long in the same position. Then came days when it was too hot to concentrate or the monsoons stole his ease. But if there were any real difficulties, he made them himself and fought them like a man playing a game of chess, with only himself as opponent.

On his eighteenth birthday, Kasper was summoned by Anouka. A child at heart, he thought perhaps she knew of his efforts and was going to reward him. He combed his hair, checked his parting, his clothes, his mind, said *I am Peace* ten times and crossed the courtyard to her room.

'Kasper,' she said. 'I've been watching you. You've been working hard.'

A modest nod.

'Very hard.'

A full bow.

'And you're a *buddhu*.'

The accusation came out in a yell that made him jump. *Buddhu* was a word he hated. It meant you were stupid, that you were going about everything in the wrong way.

'You never smile any more and you get up too early.'

He was outraged. Hadn't they gone on and on about not smiling, not showing your teeth, getting up as early as you could?

'You're to stop working in the vegetable hall.'

Kasper saw no connection between these comments. But then Anouka had never struck him as logical; sometimes he even thought her stupid.

'Also…'

Another jump.

'You're to operate the lift in the teaching block. Nine-thirty to seven, with a break in the afternoon. In a week, you'll be moved out of your room. It's time you slept in the same room as the other brothers.'

At this his chest tightened. He pictured himself being carried on a stretcher, his suitcase on top of him, as if he were a mere object being transported from one place to another.

Perhaps hearing his fear, Anouka turned to the cupboard behind her, lifted out six new sets of kurtas, and a bag of almonds which she said he was to take to the milk kitchen, soak in boiling water to soften the skin and eat before the morning class.

He disliked her intensely that day. Who needed more kurtas, and why feed him like a child? As for operating the lift, he thought this a grave insult to his intelligence. The business of sharing a room with others would just have to be endured.

Before leaving, words spilt from his mouth. 'Raj won't chop the legs off my bed, will he? Or burn it? Like he did with…'

'Of course not,' she broke in, her voice tetchy and blank. 'And here's a watch. A gift.'

'Why do I need a watch?'

'People bring all kinds of things we don't need.'

'Why?

'Stop asking questions, Kasper.'

Her reluctance to answer made him cross. Reflecting on it later, he realised that gifts in Aramani often seemed random, as if the giver were simply off-loading unwanted booty provided by sponsors or donors or visitors. Perhaps, he now wondered, the watch had even been from his mother, brought from London as a gift. He had never made any sense of the mix of high wealth and simplicity that characterised Aramani. All he knew was that this object – solid, heavy, silver – held for a few moments in the palm of his hand wiped out his fear.

He walked into the courtyard to examine it.

It was nothing like the simple Sekonda he had been given for his sixth birthday, which broke less than a year after he had worn it. The make of this watch was Rolex, pronounced in his mind as rollics. It meant nothing to him, but he liked the sound of the word when he said it out loud. He was charmed by its two gleaming hands, slim and definitive. But the third hand, which didn't stop even when he fiddled with the crown, made him uneasy.

He decided he wouldn't wear the watch on his wrist. The slim coloured bangles from the village were better: cheap but light, their colours vivid and varied. Still, he would keep the watch in his pocket and look at its face on the hour. And with that, began an involvement with time, a system of measurement he had so obstinately avoided during the early years of his life in Aramani, unless it involved food.

That afternoon, he went to the dining room and sat at an empty table, watch and notebook before him and reshaped the day, dividing the coming week into hours and minutes. He drew dots and squares beside significant moments, starting each day in the middle of the night and ending it after midnight. Seven days, each with fifteen significant pauses, made a hundred and five opportunities to think about a concept of importance from

The Philosophy. These, he would cover in his last week of freedom before being moved from his room.

While battles raged in the outside world, Kasper inhabited a world that contained its own succession of battles, which he dealt with in the same way he had faced problems as a small child: with physical exercise.

Each evening, he walked around Yanna Lake in the manner of Viraj, although twice as fast. Now and then he broke into a run, doing with his body what he wanted for his mind – to speed it towards clarity and flight – until he remembered again that slowness and repetition, not speed, were the touchstones of The Philosophy. With great effort, he began moving differently, head down, from time to time perching on a rock to capture in drawing what he had just been thinking, as if he were a lepidopterist pinning butterflies to card.

One night he fell asleep in the meditation room. At three the next morning, he was found flat on his front, forehead against the white-sheeted floor. It was concluded that he had fainted again and two brothers, themselves up early, slung him between them and carried him to the infirmary. At first he was furious, feeling the whole week was now wasted. But then he found he was glad to be back with the nurse who had looked after him as a child.

For a week he allowed himself to be cherished: small dishes of food; silence; the smell of clean sheets and flowers. He hadn't slept as long for over a year and, when he woke after a final long night, he felt he was someone else entirely.

Returning to his room, he was shocked into another

strangeness. His clothes, notebooks and drawing pads, all his pencils, even his clock had disappeared.

He knelt down and touched the legs of his bed, one after the other, then shook the watch in his pocket up and down in search not of a device to measure time but of love.

19

There were fourteen beds in his new dormitory. Between each stood a small locker and against the two spare walls, a couple of large wardrobes, three shelves allocated to each sleeper. The beds nearest the door belonged to the twins from the milk kitchen. So close were they that, had they wished, they could have held hands through the night. The other brothers were a muddle of men who struck Kasper, in his manufactured delicacy, as huge and excessively physical. Even their silence was loud.

Alarm clocks rang through the small hours, figures crept about in the dark. Beds were made so tightly it looked as if they had never been slept in at all. And there were only two bathrooms and one iron.

The business of the bathroom was the worst of the ordeal. If he didn't take a bath before meditating, he would be breaking a rule; if he did, he would be late. And thus his digestion suffered, as did his happiness.

There were other more unpleasant moments when men muscled into his happiness and broke it. The time, for example, when he was ironing and four brothers shoved at him to hurry when he couldn't go faster because the iron wasn't hot and their fury remained unspoken because:

The voicing of harsh words is against the law.

But their bodies did the speaking. And the longer he took, the angrier they became. In the end, a brother as large as a mountain snatched the iron from him, lifted it high above the table and told him he would iron Kasper's kurtas himself. With the full weight of his torso behind him, he stretched across the table and slammed the iron down hard. Kasper wanted to shout that it was the force of his body that had pressed his kurta bottoms flat. But he thought of all he had built inside him which only calmness could protect.

Another day, he had a bad time in the bathroom, and the same group of men pounded on the door to hurry him. After that, Kasper prowled about Aramani looking for a bathroom of his own.

If it was a volatile lifestyle it was also exciting. With such a mix of adults about him, each day was a risk. In an attempt at self-preservation and by observing silence, he lived as high up in his mind as he could. Early morning was the time he was able most easily to be silent. If he found silence then, he could find it the whole day through; if not, he was stuck with the battle for survival that was the crowd.

When he became weary of the stretch, he studied the picture books he'd brought from London. While he would have liked to copy the illustrations, as he had when the bedroom was his alone, the only place where it was safe to read now was in the milk kitchen.

Indifferent to rules, the twins had continued to keep his chair free for him. Sometimes he would read and look at pictures while they worked. To the sound of their songs, he tried to make sense of the hardest of his books – *The Wind in The Willows*, a title he liked for its sound though he thought Willows a place not a tree. Sometimes, when they stopped singing, they'd ask him to read to them in English. And they would laugh at his sing-song rendering of *Where the Wild Things Are*, and imitated the pictures by dancing with their arms in the air, fingers splayed wide, feet stamping. And finally, like a writer freed from his own nagging act of creation and involved in someone else's instead, he relaxed.

Refreshed, he would return to The Philosophy, kicking it about in his head like a ball. His first experiment was to play devil's advocate and list all the objections an intelligent rationalist might raise. Not that he had any experience of such a person. He had only the vaguest understanding of the world's major religions. But he'd met religious devotees in Aramani and noticed how, in their love of debate, they always seemed unhappy.

For a week he put to the test The Philosophy's theory that time moved in a cycle and one evening, sitting on the east bank of Yanna Lake, he conducted a dialogue with himself on the matter: And so, learned Philosopher, how long is this cycle of time? It doesn't matter. Yes, it does. No, it doesn't. Why not? Because a cycle goes on forever. That's why it's a cycle. But how long does it take for one cycle to end and another to begin? All numbers are symbols. That's just an excuse. No it's not. It's like nature. That isn't measured by time. Yes, it is. No, it isn't. Well, the monsoon always happens in July. Not always.

The *not always* troubled him but he persisted.

Next he interrogated celibacy. About this, he felt

87

strangely clear and in one of his notebooks described it in his own, most grown-up words:

> Important peeple have been borne many times before. They have had numrous relashunships so they need a brake from involvment.

Unconcerned about his spelling, he was pleased with this explanation for it appealed to the crux of his personality, which always sought escape from the face-to-face life that is people.

He wasn't as at ease when it came to explaining the act of sex itself. He had no adult understanding of what it involved, although he knew what it felt like in his body. Indeed, one night he had woken to the sound of two men moving in the bed next to his. Fumbling to find a torch from his bedside drawer, he shone it in the direction of the bodies beside him, studying them from beneath the protection of his sheet.

The action, quick and violent, was followed by a hissed whisper, 'What do you think you're doing?'

'Reading about the wild things.'

'Well forget the wild things and go back to sleep.'

'You're like the wild things. They're busy at night.'

'*Cupa raho!*'

He was as shocked by being told to shut up as he was by what he had seen, for both carried a violence he had met only once in Aramani – in his fight with Raj.

The next morning, he moved mechanically through his routine, listened to nothing that was said in the class, and even missed breakfast. Once in the lift, he tried to recover. For there being no lectures that morning, he stopped on the third floor, sat on the stool in the corner and, safely enclosed, took out his notebook and re-read the page which explained why lust was wrong:

> It is wrong because if one person enters another, it is not just the x that enters the y but also the minds that become miksed up together so that the inveyded is no longer himself and the inveyder isn't eyether when the hole point of Aramani is to become singerler.

At the time, he never stopped to observe that he had assigned no gender to the act he considered nor asked himself what this might mean. Instead, the insight calmed him, and he decided that if ever lust troubled him again, he would just re-read the page in his notebook where he had recorded it.

20

After years of being greedy for Aramani's food, it was around the time of his nineteenth year that Kasper began to be fussy, liking, as with colours, only to deal with one dish at a time: rice or dhal or vegetables, and then only a few mouthfuls of each. He couldn't bear watching the other brothers shovelling down their food. Worse, he became irritable when residents discussed The Philosophy over meals, as if it were merely a topic for casual conversation.

Then there was the time that the brother who had barged in on his ironing posited the view that the pictures of Gayan were superfluous: 'It's not him we're here to worship.' It was Kasper's first experience of dissent and it frightened him as much as it had as a small child to see its opposite – the zeal with which residents danced around Gayan in the courtyard, their movements becoming more and more frenzied, until one evening a sister had fallen to the ground in a lump.

'She's gone into trance,' Kala had called out, like a matron calming down a bunch of unruly children. In order to quell his own fear, he had sneezed in her face then scrambled his way down to the village where he clung hard to the water pump.

Such troubles dispelled fast. One minute he suffered,

the next what had upset him was forgotten so that in the end he no longer knew what a real trouble was. On the day that he heard Gayan's role being questioned, he marched straight to Anouka. She was outside her room in the sun, her head being rubbed. The image of two women absorbed in a small, homely act of nurture was almost sufficient to relax him. But he had a specific request and he must make it fast.

'I want to go back to my old room.'

'Why?'

This stumped him. Having lived for so long following orders, he had no idea what it meant to negotiate. Besides, something deep in his nature was against the business of snitching. So, without thinking to mention the carnal act he had witnessed, he talked about how the men's snoring made it hard to sleep, then the problem of the bathroom.

'I'll ask Gayan,' Anouka said, and let her head fall back into the cupped hands of her servant.

It wasn't the first time he had felt that, while she had loved him as a young boy, she now found him a nuisance, and he wondered if he'd done the right thing in approaching her.

No need to worry. The following day, Anouka summoned him and asked the name of the brothers who snored. When he listed them, she responded instantly that he could move back to his old room as soon as he pleased.

Then: 'What size are your feet?'

He had no idea about his feet, didn't care about his feet, only his room and the silence it promised. She handed him a pair of brown, leather walking shoes, punched with small holes. Dutifully he tried them on.

'Take them,' she said.

'But aren't they Gayan's?'

'They belonged to your father. '

Having been given what he'd asked for, as well as this strange reminder of London, Kasper felt uneasy, as if the transition to freedom had been too smooth and thus given without love. And when he carried out an inspection of his mind, he found that the high room inside him was closed. Nor could he find his watch. Perhaps, he deduced, if you were given one gift another disappeared. It didn't occur to him to wonder whether the Rolex had been stolen.

Settled again in his childhood bed, his mood lifted. He felt he would be able to study again, as well as draw and get up early. And so, once more, the word 'I' took precedence. As absorbed in themselves as he, nobody questioned him. But his body had known. For the harder he worked the more it rebelled, to the point where whole days were spent lying flat and he could think of nothing but the pain in his back, and the pain had been a relief and its stopping another relief.

Once, when the spasms were particularly severe, there was a sharp knock on the door.

'No. No one come in. I don't want to see anyone.'

'It's me. Amba.'

'I don't want to see anyone.'

'I'm not anyone,' Amba said, walking in and lying on the floor.

'What are you doing?'

'I'm showing you an exercise that will help your back. Now you do it. You lie on the floor.'

'It's cold.'

'*Buddhu!*'

The word spurred him on to do as Amba instructed.

'Now lift your left leg. Keep it there. And your right. Now do bicycles.'

'What about scooters?'

No laughter.

'I can't go on.'

'Never say that, Kasper. They're not words you should use in Aramani. Anyway, it will strengthen your spine to do some exercise. Much more than lying in bed.'

And feeling guilty about the refuge he sought in rest, Kasper had copied him.

'Now keep your legs in the air and stretch up your arms.'

Kasper waved his hands like fins.

'Not like that. Up, up! Higher!'

Just what he said to his mind: *Higher, higher!*

'Now we're going for a ride.'

While Kasper usually took orders from Amba in good heart, that day he longed for his friend to go away, for him not to be waiting outside his room while he dressed. But he had the sinking feeling he had come to know well: that there was nothing he could do to avoid what lay ahead, and that if he just did as he was told it might not be as bad as he expected.

First, green rainbow water from one of Amba's jars. Then off, up and down the mountain paths, eyes closed, letting himself be taken, finally free of a pain which was only a sob that had moved from his eyes to his spine. If they'd fallen from the scooter, tumbled to the ground and been hurt, that too would have been merely another sob, for sob was just a different word for fall.

But when he opened his eyes, they were far from the road that led down the mountain. Instead, Amba had parked in what looked like a village of huts built round an outcrop of rock shaped like a camel's double hump.

'Where are we?'

Amba beckoned him to follow.

'My massage place.'

'What's massage?'

'It's a therapy. Everyone in Aramani sits still for too long.'

They were inside an almost bare room in the middle of which was what looked like an operating table with a hole at one end.

'Take off your clothes.'

Kasper gawped.

'Now lie face down on the bed. I won't hurt you. I'm going to help you. I'll go out while you get ready.'

For what?

Kasper's mind went berserk. The brother in the dormitory, his theory about lust, the needs of his young body...

To calm himself, he kept moving, sitting, standing, going up to the wall on which hung posters of feet and hands, covered with lines and labels. Then, aware of a great exhaustion filling even the high room inside him, he gave in, stripped down to his underwear and lay down.

Returning to the room, Kasper expected only to see Amba but there was also a sallow-skinned woman in a crimson sari.

'Who are you?'

'I do the massage.'

Asserting a silence upon the room, the woman covered Kasper's body with a towel and started clicking her tongue. Then there were hands on his back, moving at speed up and down his spine in small slaps, fists twisting into his shoulders and buttocks. Through the hole in the bed, Kasper looked down at the floor and stared. When the hands that pummelled softened to a stroke, his eyes closed and he no longer knew where he was.

For how many minutes or hours he was gone, or where his mind had been, he had no idea, but it seemed to be somewhere where dreams or guilt weren't.

'Better?' she asked, passing Kasper a dressing gown and a cup of steaming tea. Kasper nodded, although he was shocked to find that in some recess of himself he also felt disappointed that it was she who had touched him, not Amba.

21

The next day marked the beginning of Holi, a festival which involved tipping buckets of coloured water over whoever you wished, either to love or to forgive. As a child, Kasper had enjoyed this day more than any other. Now that he was a serious student he rejected it as trivial.

'You must learn to be light, Kasper, to play as you used to,' Amba told him.

'Playing is for children.'

'Sometimes it is; sometimes it isn't.'

Kasper knew his friend was right, knew he'd become too dogged. But with his back free of pain he wanted only to return to his studies.

'Go on, study then,' said Amba. 'You've got the whole day. I'll tell you the plan tomorrow.'

Again he gave in, as if he half knew that holding himself so high was dangerous; it would be wiser to let himself be knocked sideways so that his mind, like his back, could relax.

Kneeling in his tool shed Amba stirred red dye into a bucket of water.

'Come on, help me with this,' he said. 'It's for Kala.'

'Why Kala?'

'I'm sick of her, that's why. Telling everyone what to do. If you study she's cross; if you don't study she's cross. She deserves it.'

Kasper was surprised by his friend's tone. He had taken him to a land of green sun-water and love; now he was taking him towards hurt.

'You said you didn't want to be a child anymore so I'm going to help you grow up.'

What was that supposed to mean? That growing up involved unkindness? He knew that wasn't true. It was only that Amba was blessed with the quality of balance: as at ease with the mess of dislike, as he was with the neatness of belief, whereas Kasper had lost all perspective, fighting off the least negativity as if it had the power to kill.

He was bewildered when Amba started issuing instructions: 'Get into the lift, take Kala and Anouka with you, then follow them out, give these flowers to Anouka and walk her a little way from Kala so that I have time to pour the red water all over her and avoid Anouka.'

'I can't.'

'Why not?'

'I don't want to be involved.'

Amba looked up at him. 'That's your trouble, Kasper. Your fear of involvement.'

Stung, he gave in, and they played the trick after all. But just as he was manoeuvring Kala into position, Gayan appeared and, seeing what was coming, he rushed Kala out of the way so that the water only reached the hem of her sari.

Amba pounded down the stairs.

'Typical!'

'Typical what?'

'Typical Gayan. And it's time you knew.'

'Knew what?'

'Don't be upset, Kasper, but if other people know, you should know too.'

'Before Aramani, Gayan was married to Kala. It was a long time ago, and they don't live as man and wife anymore, but that's why he rescued her, even from Holi.'

'So Raj is Gayan's son?'

'Yes.'

At this, Kasper burst into tears.

It was outrage and confusion that made him behave as he did on the second evening of Holi.

Once again, he had been chosen to dress up as a prince: silk tunic, sash, jewels, crown, cloth-covered chappals. While he took sensual pleasure in the texture of silk and the feel of soft colours, he detested the public nature of the event, also its pointlessness. Seated on the stage, he hunted desperately for Amba or Bhani or the twins.

Instead there was Gayan, a married man, but not in the way his father in London was married. For him, life had been a hurried, hardworking matter, whereas Gayan seemed perpetually refreshed as if nothing either irritated or excessively pleased him. Anger burned. The costume he wore was restricting; the crown in particular made his head itch. His thoughts started racing. He liked to meditate unobserved, not in public. And why should he sit for such a long time when half the audience was dozing?

In the end, pushed to the limit of his tolerance, he slipped out from the end of the row and left the room.

Once in the fresh air he yanked off the swathes of stiff, gold material. Only habit and the fear that if he left his costume strewn about the courtyard he would be found out, made him take the time to fold it, shove it under the mustard-coloured sofa in the little visitors' room to one side of the courtyard, then run again to his room where he changed.

Back in his kurtas, he immediately felt better. His half-English body, which had in its cellular memory the freshness of fields and sea and the woodland paths of England, darted out of Aramani and down the hill to Yanna Lake.

The road that circled Yanna was quiet. He breathed freely and relaxed, enjoying the slap of his chappals against the road. As always, he looked up at the sky for its space. A mistake. In the few seconds when he wasn't concentrating, a car sped towards him, headlights accusingly bright. With windows down, music blared from the radio as the car came to a skid halt.

A head appeared. 'All right, brother?'

Noise and laughter turned the word brother into an insult: Brother! You think you're my spiritual brother? I hate your guts if you want to know. That was what the voice meant, for it belonged to Raj, the boy who had previously belonged to himself alone but had turned suddenly into the son, not just of Kala but also of Gayan.

Although he had been sad at his mother's departure from Aramani, it had taken Kasper little time to forget her.

Whenever a letter had arrived he had stored it in the bag under his bed and returned to his sketchpad. Whatever she had written, to his high, mean mind she was a traitor who had abandoned their way of life to look after a sick man she didn't even love. When news came that it was she who had died, not his father, he had felt nothing.

Three days after the news, a ceremony was held. A small group led by Gayan, Anouka and Viraj processed down to Yanna where they scattered flowers on the water like ashes. Standing beside Gayan as the petals floated and crumpled, Kasper looked down at his teacher's feet, as if the shoes he was wearing, so solid and brown, were the only things fit to steady his heartbeat. He had come away from the ceremony high on his own dignity. To be like the Elders and show no emotion, even better to feel none, would surely be considered an achievement.

That evening, Gayan had called Kasper to his room, placed his hands on the boy's shoulders and said, 'Sorrow has its place, Kasper. Don't be ashamed of it.'

So gently did he speak these unfamiliar words that instead of retorting that The Philosophy instructed against sorrow, Kasper felt a pang of intense pain, as if his emotional self had suddenly been awakened from a long sleep.

'I want you to take on a new duty, Kasper. Every morning, you're to go to the post room, collect the letters written by the foreigners and read them. If what they write is serious, bring them to me. If their questions are trivial, give them to Viraj.'

The instruction was flummoxing. Didn't Gayan know that he still only had the reading age of an eight-year-old? Was he inattentive or was he trying to tell him he

100

was important? If important, why did the task feel like a punishment?

'I don't want anything to do with upset people.'

'It's our job to help those who have fallen.'

'Why me though?'

At this, Gayan looked down at his hands in silence.

Kasper was helpless in the face of such authority. And so, each morning before going to the lift he would walk to the post room, take all the letters with foreign stamps, leave them in his room unopened, only returning to them in the evening when he flicked through them briefly.

If he was pleased that he could understand more of their contents than he expected, he also considered them ridiculous:

Can I meditate lying down or do I have to sit up?

Last week, I ate an egg.

How do I still do my job when I have to get up so early?

I have had a backache for three years.

This last letter, he hurled across the room for it read as a criticism of his own physical pain.

Swiftly he sought refuge in a plan. He would do as he had been told, but only in part. He would ration how many letters he delivered. While hundreds arrived in the post room, he would collect them all but deliver only ten a fortnight: four to Gayan and six to Viraj.

Ten. The number, as a small child, he had wished always to score in a test.

22

Looking back, Kasper wondered again about his job as postmaster. Had it been assigned in order to loosen his commitment to Aramani, even to drive him away? And why hadn't he passed the letters on as he'd been told to? In fact, now that he thought about it, he realised that the letters were at the root of everything that was wrong.

With him.

With his selfishness.

With Aramani.

And his mother? Kasper had never really thought much about her after she'd returned to London. While he supposed he must still love her in one way or another, when he thought of her, he skated over the image as if, with her in mind, the ground beneath him might crack and a hole appear into which he would fall and lose himself.

Until now.

Now she seemed to be both pushing him away and forcing him to face the fact that something she had begun was unfinished. For who was she, deep down, this woman who had so blithely left her husband in London then returned so suddenly for no apparent reason?

Back in his room all these years later, Kasper was viscerally aware of the woman as she had been, her hands in particular, with their beautiful fingers that had seemed always to be flicking material, doing up buttons, folding and fiddling and tidying. Her body itself had somehow come to be merged with the elegant fall of her sari, so that there were no longer bare arms and gardening, stretching up to cupboards, caresses, hugs, kisses... Instead there was washing and scrubbing, washing and scrubbing, dressing, undressing and dressing again, until not even her wrists were visible, and never her legs.

Looking at his own slim adult form, Kasper wondered if he too had, in some way, dematerialised. Even now his body didn't look quite solid. He had braved a few fitness sessions in Amsterdam from which he had taken some pleasure. But when he had tried working out in London, he'd found the gym, with its crude black equipment, repulsive. So instead he'd begun running, pounding the streets, willing himself to become more resilient. The evidence of this effort was visible in the strong muscles of his thighs. The rest of his body bore the stamp of his early existence, which had left so much of life out.

With this reflection upon his past, and how it had been both rich and yet somehow not there at all, Kasper moved to the middle of the room and stared at the small, glass-topped table on which the same vase of flowers stood as had been there when he'd arrived in Aramani at the age of seven. Fingering the fake, blue cotton petals he felt a surge of disgust.

Back in the lift, Kasper suffered another collision with Mina – the woman who was floored by floors. With no way to escape the lift, her spillage of words was doubly irritating: how her husband was a businessman; how their main house was in Bombay, close to the sea; how he often worked in Europe, sometimes Amsterdam, other times London – 'he was in London recently, which is why we are here.' This seemed to Kasper an unnecessarily detailed account, from which she moved on to say that she was interested to know when he had begun operating the lift, and did he not find it dull spending all day going up and down?

When she reached her eighth statement and fourth question, he snapped at her to be quiet. To which she replied that she would be delighted if he would visit her and her husband on their balcony for tea, they were staying in the accommodation block on the road leading to Yanna Lake. This so astonished him that, weakened by anguish, he found himself agreeing.

You do not live for yourself. Life is lived through you.

You are responsible for everything you do.

Always say yes and life will reward you.

Rule after rule, each contradicting the other, until he longed to stick a needle in his arm and sedate himself.

The confusion of colours that greeted him as he reached the couple's balcony both reflected and calmed his mood, for they seemed to have turned it into an outdoor sitting room: chairs draped with quilts and cushions; on the table a silver tea set that they must have brought with them, unless there was a new storage space in Aramani containing such extravagances; also a bowl of fruit.

'I don't understand the place,' Mina said. 'Perhaps you could explain it.'

Kasper gazed at the fruit.

'Do help yourself. I mean, you're an attractive young man. Don't you want to get married?'

'Married?'

'Yes, married.'

Despite experiences during his time away from Aramani, the word marriage spoken here on this balcony, by this woman, overlooking Yanna Lake, sounded as unnatural as it had when Amba had talked of it all those years ago.

'Leave the boy alone, Mina.'

'Well, what's wrong with loving your wife, that's what I'd like to know?'

'You see she's really interrogating me not you.' Balvan's tone was greasily conspiratorial.

In the past, Kasper would have enjoyed flaunting his celibacy, as well as explaining its reasons. He would also have exited fast any scene which asked him to take sides. But wasn't that what he was here for? To take a side, a stand, make a statement of intention, if only to himself.

'People must do as they wish,' was the extent of his response. Then he changed the subject, asking what had brought the couple to Aramani in the first place. Mina glanced questioningly at her husband, who swiftly explained that he had business nearby and they had also come to Aramani for a holiday.

'I find Aramani peaceful. Mina is bored by it.'

Balvan raised his arm and gestured to the mountain

view. On his wrist Kasper noticed a Rolex watch identical to the one Anouka had given him when he was eighteen. Seeing Kasper stare, he said, 'This? One doesn't need such a thing here. Time in Aramani seems unimportant.'

'Why do you wear it then?'

'In the West, it's useful to tell the time. This one came from Dubai.'

'Dubai?'

'Dubai.'

For some reason the word's harsh sounding consonants put a stop to Kasper's questions. Who cared about the watch? He didn't need it or like it or miss the one that had mysteriously disappeared from the dormitory, or even want to think about it, lest it was possible that his mother had brought it as a gift that hadn't been valued.

'Anyway,' interjected Mina. 'Tell us more about Aramani.'

'I know very little about the place. If you want a detailed explanation go to the courtyard. Sit there and the right person will tell you what you want to know.'

'If you know so little about the place how do you know about the courtyard?'

'Stop harassing the poor boy.' Balvan's eyes bulged from the huge frog of his face. 'The food is excellent anyway. Look at this fruit. Do take it all. We bought the oranges specially for you.'

For a second time, Kasper's mind went pale. The lift. Oranges. Punishment. Reward...

'Yes, they employ very skilled cooks.' There was no heart in his voice. Barely even thought.

'But you said everyone worked here voluntarily,' Mina bullied. Balvan looked at Kasper as if to say: What can you do, she's always as bad?

'They do work here for nothing.'

He heard himself spieling an edited version of his own story. 'I've come here voluntarily myself, from London.' At this, he looked at Mina. 'But only to operate the lift and I'm only here for a few weeks. Like you, for a holiday.'

> *Lie once and you will lie over and over until you won't even recognise what truth is.*

The Philosophy again, rushing in on him just when he both needed and least wanted it. For today, he felt bored of lofty searches for the truth. Still, the slogan felt right while it struck him, as they sat in the brightness of the afternoon, that all three of them were lying.

23

There had come a time in his young life when Kasper began using the lift as a place in which to hide. Seated in the corner, black hair fiercely parted, he became dismissive. For the visitors were insatiable, and would have broken into his high room had he let them. It was to protect himself, as well as to become the embodiment of The Philosophy, that he also started regarding the lift as a symbol for his own spiritual ascent. Deep down, he knew it was ridiculous, this transforming of one thing into another, so that he interpreted an innocent person asking him to return the lift to the ground floor as the sign of a mistake. But for as long as he made things into ideas the visitors couldn't touch him. Even his name became obsolete. By the age of twenty, he was known by residents, visitors and even the villagers only as *Liftman*.

If someone were to sit him down and ask when in his life he had been happiest, he would have said: When I was known only as Liftman, as if, in that phase, he was in touch with the whole world while having to see none of it. He no longer went on rides with Amba; festivals, he shunned entirely. Time, too, began to move as if by his own instruction. Seconds stretched into minutes, minutes to hours and before sleeping, he noted down his errors.

Cruel and proud, he knew the names of no visitor, while each knew his. Walking to the dining room to take tea, crossing the courtyard or slipping into a meditation room, he was aware he was being studied and copied and if he caught a person's eye, he used his mind to stand theirs to attention. Anyone who complicated matters or lost their confidence he ignored.

In time, the Westerners began not only to come to the lift in order to talk to him, they also followed him round the lake, running up to him with the enthusiasm of children, wanting to know why Gayan kept himself to himself, why The Philosophy asserted that time was cyclical and why heaven was said to exist only in India. Why, too, they wanted to know, had the whole of their lives turned into a competition? On and on they went until he would conjure up a slogan or the quick snap of silence, not to help them, but be free of them.

Late morning; high summer.

Kasper was drawing Banhi as she dozed outside her fruit store. Just as he was reaching her hands, knuckly and gnarled in her lap, a message came saying Gayan wished to see him. Annoyed that his drawing would have to be discarded, he inwardly sighed. For if one could escape almost anything in Aramani a summons from Gayan was the exception.

As he entered the cottage, the old man was seated, a glass of iced tea on the silver gilt table beside him. Kasper consoled himself with the thought that one day he would make a painting of the room: table, chair, bed close against the wall, black and white spotted quilt, blue embroidered rug, arranged in perfect combination…

He took in the coolness, the fragrance of jasmine and sage, the sepia prints of old Bombay houses… 'A gift from an old friend who had them specially designed for the room,' Gayan had told him once. Finally, faced with his high room in more lavish form, he looked closely at Gayan: that bowed head, a pile of folded papers in his lap.

'I'd like you to conduct classes for the studio directors.'

'Me?'

'Yes. You're our best student.'

'Why give classes only to the directors?'

'The directors are the most important.'

'Why?'

'If the directors aren't taught properly, how will their students learn?'

Kasper retorted more defiantly than intended that Gayan had always insisted that all humans were equal so why was he now saying that only the directors should be taught?

'Everyone receives the reward they deserve in the end.'

Kasper was baffled by the non-sequitur but, like a child fighting the worn-out values of a parent, he persisted.

'In the end maybe but what about now? Shouldn't we treat people fairly now? Isn't fairness what we stand for?'

'Kasper, you think too much.'

These words offended him to the core. What did it mean, telling a person that they think too much? It was what he was thinking that Gayan didn't like. So in a rush of objection he told him that he would either teach everyone or no one. Then he walked out, empowered, because suddenly he felt he had taken Aramani into his own hands and as its 'best student' restored it to its truth.

But minutes after the meeting, he noticed he was bolting down his lunch as if he had just made a hole in himself and was filling it with food. Once finished, he spotted Viraj in the courtyard, an empty chair beside him. Kasper joined him, longing for the old man to speak a few words of reassurance. Instead, he simply lay his newspaper on his lap, stared up at the mountains that circled Aramani in a mist-covered crown and resumed reading.

That day, it struck Kasper that perhaps when Viraj took his walks around the lake, he wasn't thinking about The Philosophy at all; he was only walking for its own sake, just as now he was doing nothing more than reading his newspaper in the sun.

The next afternoon Kasper returned to Gayan.

He was seated in exactly the same place, head still bowed, as if he'd been waiting all night and day for the scene to resume.

Kasper said his name.

No response.

'What are you doing in your head, Gayan?'

'I am doing what I do every spare second and minute of my day. I'm praying.'

'But you don't teach us to pray.'

'There are times when it's necessary. I'm sorry, Kasper. You're right about the directors. Let anyone come to the classes.'

Rather than being pleased, Kasper felt as if in the space of a moment Gayan had both made him whole then broken him again, so that his world was a place with no landmarks. Perhaps seeing his worry, Gayan stretched out his hand and, rather than using words of consolation, stared deep into his eyes.

> *Stay with the father and you will always be protected.*
> *Leave and you fall.*

24

Small spaces compress and intensify thought. The walls of the lift in which Kasper now spent most of his day seemed to bounce memories back to him so that Aramani as it was in the present paled in comparison with his memory of how it had been. Balvan and Mina kept interrupting him, often entering the lift together.

One morning Mina asked if he would be kind enough to accompany them to the village and suggest the most reputable tailors. Kasper hadn't been to the village since his arrival and didn't much want to go now, although he longed for the simple pleasures it had once brought him – the donkey, the cows, the kindness of the bangle-seller.

'We'd be so grateful,' said Mina with a directness that struck him as genuine. 'This afternoon? After your shift ends? We could take tea as we did before and then go once the sun has cooled. What do you say?'

'No, Mina, the poor boy's busy. We can take a quick chai in the village if we get thirsty. Let's only steal an hour of his time. If you would be so kind.'

Kasper realised he had no choice but to *be so kind* and was no longer surprised by the way Balvan kept referring to him as a boy. It struck him as an insult nonetheless, reminding him once more of the fact that, even at twenty-seven, in the world's terms, he still hadn't grown up.

Together they walked past the kitchens and across the riverbed to the camp where brightly-dressed women were hanging out their washing. As usual the children cried out for money. Kasper watched them closely. A small girl and her brother were making a colony out of earth. He bent down beside them as he had as a child. The girl's skin was crusted with salt, her eyes covered in the same film as Banhi's. Perhaps she too had cataracts? But to Kasper it seemed as if he was staring straight into tears. Although he had no idea how to talk to children, he longed to lift the little boy into his arms and hug him. Instead, he tried patting him on the head; the child brushed him away like another fly.

'Do you think you'll stay here forever?' asked Balvan, as they resumed walking.

The words hit his heart like a rock.

'I'm only a guest.'

'Yes, yes I've heard that theory of Gayan's that we are all guests in this world. A very good way to live. But what about in practical terms? Will you stay here for long?'

Once more Kasper was irritated, as if he'd been tricked into being alone with this couple simply in order to be interrogated.

'I'll go when I'm ready.'

'I don't think it's a place for a young man like you. The world should be travelled.'

While Kasper had heard these words before, there was an indifference to the way Balvan spoke them, as if he had moved slowly around the planet filling himself with delicacies, learning nothing from the places he had seen.

Once on the flat of the road, they passed the water

114

pump and the spot near the bank where the taxi drivers dropped their passengers. They made a curious trio, moving down the hill into the small teeming streets of the village. And for the second time in their company and amid so much colour and activity, Kasper found himself feeling better.

When they saw a tailor Kasper knew to be skilled, they were welcomed effusively into the shop with its white-sheeted floor.

'Come, come, come, yes, brother, Mataji, Babaji, here, yes, here please....'

Mina eased herself down onto an upholstered footstool, Balvan and Kasper hovering about while she demanded silk, cotton, material for a nightdress, a sari, a petticoat, a headscarf... Her eyes wandered to sheets, pillowcases, rugs. Focusing on the young tailor, Kasper couldn't help being drawn to his form as he stretched up with a long-handled hook to bring down roll after roll of material until Mina sat like a queen – a sea of bright fabric at her feet, her gold-bangled wrists tinkling, hands flicking, touching, discarding, selecting...

Kasper had always loved the colour white against the bright reds and greens of nature. But the patterns on the fabrics had an equivalent beauty. There was something comforting, too, in being surrounded by so much cloth. Balvan, on the other hand, became impatient. The child assistant was ordered to bring tea while Kasper took out his sketchpad and drew the young tailor, as if this would make him impervious to the offer of refreshment. For having drunk and eaten many a meal in Europe, he hesitated to accept tea here in the village. He had never eaten or drunk anything here except water. Perhaps his irritation showed for after Mina had finally completed her purchases, Balvan patted Kasper on the back and said, 'I'd like to buy you a gift. For your room perhaps?'

'It's not my room,' Kasper said, though he was troubled by the idea of it being anyone else's.

'A quilt,' chirped Mina. 'I'm going to buy a quilt.' Balvan tutted as they moved on to a shop where quilts were stored floor to ceiling in rolls of bright colour. And Kasper knew then that he was going to say yes; he was sick of the blankets and his bed was hard.

Do not accept gifts.

But I don't live in Aramani anymore. I'm a free man. If my room is comfortable, I'll feel better.

And he thought of the nights when he had wanted to stay up but the cold had robbed him of willpower.

Mina was delighted by his gratitude and Balvan organised for the packages to be carried back to Aramani by the tailor's assistant. When they reached the gates and Kasper took the quilt into his own arms, he had the feeling that, having accepted their gift, he would never be able to shake the couple off.

'Liftman, I'll tell the bangle-seller I've seen you,' shouted the tailor's assistant as he ran back towards the village.

That evening, Kasper missed supper, went straight to his room and unrolled the two quilts, spreading one under the bottom sheet, the other on top of the blanket. Immediately the place seemed changed in the way Hanneke had been able with such ease to turn a bare room into a place of beauty and style.

Hanneke.

The girl from Amsterdam who on a summer day in 1983 had strolled into his life just when he'd had it summed up most neatly: body at peace, mind undisturbed, drawings more assured. He had even transformed his life in the lift, satisfying visitors' questions by handing them, as they entered, slogans he'd illustrated on small cards so that they'd leave feeling they hadn't simply been transported from one floor to another but had had their spirits raised too.

On the morning he met Hanneke, the card he had picked for his next passenger stated that we arrive in the world naked and leave it naked. When it was she who appeared, with her blonde hair cropped as short as a boy's, he had dropped the entire pack of cards on the lift floor.

For several days he didn't see her again but he thought about her more than he intended. He excused this in himself by integrating her into his treasure store of images; she wasn't a beautiful human being, she wasn't even female. She was patience, introversion, independence, self-respect – symbols only – just as his lift was a symbol. But symbols don't cause yearning and he yearned for Hanneke.

In Aramani, what you think about manifests. Three days later, as he was walking to the dining room for lunch, Kasper saw her in the courtyard. She wasn't wearing the uniform usually assigned to women, but kurta pyjamas just like his own. Briefly she turned to him and smiled.

He didn't smile back for these weren't his smiling days although something passed between them.

Another day, seated in one of the small meditation rooms, he felt a presence behind him. He didn't allow himself to turn round, instead fixing his eyes on the photo of Gayan, long-mended since his childish assault. When the atmosphere in the room became suddenly thin he knew it was she who had been seated behind him and knew, too, that she had now left.

Brushes escalated. Twice, three times a day until this girl-boy seemed to be everywhere, and everywhere, too, like an obstacle in the way of a beautiful view, were students eager for his attention. Thirstily they asked him the very questions he was asking himself: 'Liftman, what do you do if you like someone more than you should?'

'You make sure you're never in their company alone, and if it becomes too hard to bear you tell one of the Elders.'

Too hard to bear.

Yet he had told nobody.

25

One morning, during the first Philosophy class of the morning, a note was passed from the back row to the front where Kasper sat cross-legged and attentive. In it was an instruction that at four he should go to the top floor of the teaching block to meet with the students visiting from Holland.

Good.

Clear.

An order.

To be, in spite of its anonymity, obeyed.

When he entered the teaching room allocated for the meeting, he was surprised to see that the chairs were set out in a circle. All his life, chairs had been arranged in rows. By force, he drew in his mind as if he were royalty waiting to be shown where to sit. Sure enough, a chair had been covered with a white sheet and plumped-up cushion.

'Good afternoon. I am honoured to be here to address you on a topic which –'

Hanneke butted in. 'Thank you for coming, Liftman. For a while we've been wanting to talk to someone closer to our own age. We respect the Elders but they don't answer our questions. We don't want to insult them but we want to talk about some of the things we find challenging in The Philosophy.'

Hearing their softly-accented voices, the questions and answers Kasper had rehearsed as he had paced round the lake seemed suddenly redundant for he was being asked to speak from experience when the fact was he had none.

'Well, why don't you tell me more about what you find strange,' he braved, nervous of this grown-up approach to uncertainty.

One by one they spoke, some not understanding how a fixed timespan could be assigned to the life of the planet or why the length of its cycles were so precisely defined. Others spoke of more practical matters such as their dismay at the sugar-filled diet of the Elders. The most heartfelt plea came from a young woman whose father had recently died. She had loved him dearly, she said, and didn't know why, when she had asked Kala how to deal with her sorrow, she had been brushed aside with of all things laughter! 'I understand the theory,' she said, 'but when it comes to it, death isn't as they say it is here. It takes time to get over.'

'There's no such thing as death.'

The young woman lowered her head.

'The soul goes on. It never ends.'

Still the young woman said nothing.

When the meeting came to an end only Hanneke stayed behind.

'Don't worry about her. It's understandable she's sad; she's always sad. She has depression.'

Kasper had never heard of the word, didn't know

what it meant to *have* depression, to *have* anything. So he pushed the word aside, falling instead into the face of the being before him. What was it that appealed to him? The clear skin, the roundness of the face, the absolute whiteness of the kurtas, or was it just the flattery? Whatever it was, she seemed to be of a different ilk to the other visitors: less frail, less shell-shocked, a spokesperson rather than victim of the problems they expressed. And while this was, in his pride, what he had thought all visitors should be like, faced by it in the form of such an elegant being as Hanneke, he was angry.

26

If emotion had once been a passing discomfort, now back in Aramani, it seemed to flood Kasper's entire being so that, sleepless, he sensed the only answer was the shock of fresh air.

Wrapping himself in one of the quilts Mina and Balvan had bought him the day before, the gift seeming to decide his route, he left his room and made his way down the hill towards the building where the couple was staying. Within minutes he was standing on their balcony.

Taking the same chair he had sat on to drink tea, he listened to the sound of the dark. No dogs howled now and the sky was spotted with stars. Had it been warmer he might finally have managed to fall into a doze but even the quilt couldn't take the edge off the chill.

Then into the silence came words.

'Why not, Mina? We're man and wife, after all.'

'It doesn't feel right here, Bala. I'd rather the hotel.'

'Don't be absurd.'

'What about Kasper?'

'What about Kasper?'

'I was thinking about him.'

'Why? He doesn't live here anymore, don't forget. He's been in Europe for years.'

Hearing his name, something in Kasper's head seemed to snap so that he suddenly jerked forwards.

'No, Bala. I'm not in the mood.'

'Keep me warm then. These beds are so hard. We'll move to the hotel tomorrow.'

Not wanting to hear words so alien to Aramani, Kasper listened intently.

A pause.

Then laughter.

'Stop it!'

Kasper stood up, pressed his back against the balcony railings and closed his eyes.

More laughter.

Involuntarily he pictured the couple naked.

Then a cry from Mina as if to make public that the act was over.

Now he began shaking. It wasn't blame that provoked him; he had nothing to do with these people. But the mention of his name was baffling. So as fast as he could he was away from the balcony, rushing toward the stairs, the quilt in a bundle under his arm. As he went, he heard a bucket being filled, a sign that someone was up and preparing for their first meditation of the day. Of this he could make no more sense than he could of his name being mentioned by Mina. As for the thought of physical pleasure and spiritual endeavour occurring in rooms less than yards apart, that seemed utterly incongruent. For throughout everything – paradoxes, contradictions, confusions – Kasper had always succeeded in keeping Aramani distinct and unbroken.

Back in his room he finally slept, not waking until after nine. He realised it had crept up on him slowly, this streak both of restlessness and indolence. As a child he had been enlivened by joy: running, climbing, riding with Amba on his scooter, wolfing down food, all in his own time, only as it pleased him. Now he seemed filled with distress.

Looking back on those years when his intelligence was so untrammelled by experience, Kasper could see that the question and answer session with the students from Holland had marked a turning point in his life. For the first time, he was being confronted with his own ignorance. And yet that very ignorance, set as it was against a backdrop of spiritual power, was what was drawing their attention so forcefully.

A few days after the first meeting, a second was arranged. For it being held in the same room, Kasper expected it to be a repeat in the way everything was repeated in Aramani. He thus attributed too much meaning to the fact that this time the chairs were set out in rows.

Dismissing from his mind all that had concerned them at the previous gathering, he took his seat at the front and, unsolicited, talked at them about his favourite topic: the meaning of purity.

Keep everything distinct.

Don't muddle your parents with your beliefs; your jobs with your spiritual practice; divide everything up, keep it neat.

They sat silent and respectful for the length of his talk and after an hour he left, proud of his clarity, but disappointed too, as if he hadn't quite made the impression he'd hoped. On his way down the stairs, he tripped. And the next thing he knew, he was in the infirmary again, under the care of those who had looked after him as a child.

'It's a sprain. You'll have to wear this boot for the next six days at least.'

This boot was an unwieldy grey sock, so heavy that it anchored him to the ground, making him feel like an old man. And while he had always courted attention, now everyone looked at him as they did at a person who was failing.

He limped to the third meeting. This time, it was in a different room, and required of him neither wisdom nor advice. Wanting to thank him, they had brought small plates of fruit from Aramani's kitchen. Exactly the way Kasper liked food to be. But words from The Philosophy sounded out in his mind.

Do not accept gifts.

And suddenly everyone left and he was alone with the person he most wished to avoid.

'We'd like you to come to Amsterdam. We enjoy your way of explaining.'

Kasper was shocked by the confusion of feelings this compliment provoked. But what had he thought she was going to say? That she felt drawn to him, that he was always in her thoughts? He didn't acknowledge it at first; was too busy persuading himself that the invitation was an honour, that the business of his life was to teach not be flattered by a being who seemed neither man nor woman but a figure from a painting. He replied that he had no say in how he spent his time. If he were to visit Amsterdam, wherever that was, the Elders would have to be consulted.

It was only after a week of intense self-examination that Kasper forced himself to confess his feelings to Anouka. He told her of Hanneke's invitation and said he'd rather not accept. She asked him why not and he looked at her great white-clad body and threw his statement at her like a rock he was trying to break against her.

'Lust.'

Unmoved, Anouka looked into his eyes.

'Lust is for children!'

He was hurt that she didn't use his name, as if she had ceased to care. In fact, it seemed to him that they both wanted him in the dirt: Gayan rubbing his nose into people's personal anxieties by making him read letters and Anouka pushing him away from Aramani completely. Why? What had he done wrong? Why did they no longer wish to protect him when they had loved him so dearly as a child? Why, so easily, did they simply conjure from the travel office a ticket and small book?

'What's that?'

'Your passport, Kasper. It was sent from London.'

'Who by?'

'I don't know. The details have nothing to do with me.'

Kasper opened the book and saw a small photo of himself that he recognised. Amba had taken it one day, a white sheet hung behind him with two clothes pegs. At the time, Kasper hadn't asked him why he was making things so complicated but he remembered how Amba had kept telling him not to move, to stare straight at the camera, not look down or move or smile.

And that was that. Kasper was sent on his way, handkerchiefs waving at the gate to wash away tears unshed.

27

It was July 1984 when to sun on his face Kasper arrived in Amsterdam. His first time in Europe for fourteen years. There was a particular smell to the place: rain and green and metal. The relief this prompted surprised him, as if beneath the sweetness of rose petals and sage, he had been fighting off the stench of India's underbelly for as long as he could remember.

Meeting him at Schiphol airport, Hanneke placed fresh flowers of welcome in his arms. Her skin was clear, her smile so broad and open that his head felt light.

He felt more stable when, in the car, she introduced him to Henry, the brother she said would look after him – a robust-looking man with red hair.

'You'll be staying with him for the first night,' she said.

And that was another relief.

But he disliked the house with its jumble of shoes in the hallway. Henry made a joke of it, telling him they had spent hours tidying up the place before his arrival and that his first appointment was in an hour. The word 'appointment' revived him, returning him to the purpose of his visit, which was to speak of the soul and all that was safe from the business of travel and welcome and lust.

After showering, he checked himself in the mirror, mindful of the fact that he was representing Aramani so should look his best.

In the half-darkness of the hired auditorium, Hanneke stood to introduce him, her words distant for being spoken in Dutch and yet their inflexion persuasive, while his own voice caught in his throat. Speaking about Aramani was like unclothing a secret which was hard to word once away from its source. But by the end of his talk, for which he had done no preparation, as a connoisseur of silence, he sensed it had gone well; that he had succeeded in carrying the spirit of Aramani down the mountain and into the minds of his audience. Still, the discussion that followed he found disconcerting, for it was then that he was faced with questions about his childhood, a topic which he wished to avoid.

The past has passed.

At the end of the evening, Hanneke proposed a vote of thanks, after which she said that The Liftman would distribute gifts.

'But I don't have any gifts,' he whispered.

She pointed to a basket behind his chair full of small parcels. Gift-giving of this kind was an Aramani custom and so he copied the Elders who liked to stare at their recipients as if they were mending their souls at the same time as giving. When the first few members of the audience came up, he stared so long that Hanneke had to nudge him to hurry; they had only rented the venue for a few hours. While now he would perfectly understand that practicality, then he was lost in an experience of self-glorification, revelling in his superiority, seeing nothing in these people's eyes but the fact that their characters were flawed and mundane. They who nursed cancer patients, had recently lost parents, jobs, lovers, who ran marathons and banks, had written novels and articles and had children to attend to, were nothing to him. And as he lay awake that night in a bed that was so comfortable he could barely think straight, he spun mad yarns in his head about teaching the world how to think.

On his second evening, Hanneke told him that Henry would be out of town so he should stay in her flat on the top floor of an old building overlooking Prinsengracht. The flat had oak floors and, on the walls, water-colours she had painted herself. He looked at them admiringly, faced suddenly with the feeling that the posters plastered all over the walls of Aramani were crude in comparison. Here were soft washes of colour, flecks of light on water, huge skies…

'Do you like them?'

Her enquiry surprised him. She seemed so sure of herself. Feeling disloyal to his home, he nodded and moved to the window to look at the canal below. He thought of Delhi and how run-down it was: the smog and the filth and the honking of car horns, the rickshaws and bicycles, the noise and the semi-darkness even of summer days. And though he had the Indian's affection for his own country, he was impressed by this new place he had come to, while he worried about the bathroom and the food and how he would iron his clothes. More insistent than all this was The Philosophy:

> *A brother eats and sleeps next to his brother; a sister eats and sleeps next to her sister.*

For another rule being broken, their first meal together felt complicated. Kasper needed to work out how to eat one dish at a time, in silence and away from her mind, which seemed to bore into his with an intensity that unsettled him.

'Tell me, Liftman,' she said as she took his plate, 'what's your real name? I need to introduce you in a more conventional way at the next lecture.'

The question was an intrusion, hurling him back to his origins, his short life in London and also to his mother who hadn't lived long enough to know him by the title of which he was so proud.

'I'm sorry. I've offended you.'

'Not at all.'

'Is it a secret?'

'No. Yes.'

'I'm sorry.'

And like a person recovering from trauma he fell into fawning.

'Kasper. Kasper Chaudhury.'

Seeing his discomfort, she said, 'I'll introduce you as Liftman and explain why you're known by that title.'

The next morning when to the sound of the bells from Westerkerk, they sat by the window and meditated, images passed through his mind in swift succession: a ladder, a bird, a tree whose roots spread like veins under the top skin of the earth... Of these, he was able to make some sense, used as he was to the language of metaphor. But then he began rushing. A car, a river, a wall, slogans and words until his skull tightened and he found himself clutching the arms of the chair. Only after fifteen minutes was he able to regain the calmness that came with instruction:

Have faith.

Faith was a word Kasper had never much liked. Whenever he heard it, it reminded him of the muddle of emotions he felt when his mother had died and Gayan had told him to give sorrow its place. He hated sorrow, not understanding that sometimes it is the only way to slow the mind down. He hated it even more when, at the end of the hour, Hanneke looked at him with bright eyes, leant towards him, as fresh and clean-looking as the flowers she had placed in his arms at the airport, and all he could think of was that she was going to touch him, hold him, perhaps even kiss him. And he wanted it more than anything he had ever longed for in Aramani, and at the same time wanted her nowhere near him.

Love.

Detachment.

The words faced each other, giants in combat, and he knew in an instant that, if he gave in to the first, he would lose everything Aramani had built in him; if to the second, he would remain forever the mere ghost of a human being.

But she didn't touch him. Instead she leant back in her chair and in glass-calm voice asked if he would talk to the students at the studio. 'About celibacy. They're always writing letters about it. I send them to Aramani but I don't know who reads them.'

At the mention of letters, Kasper had the feeling that she knew everything about him. In fact, not just everything but more than he himself knew. His answer was self-defence not attack.

'You shouldn't be reading their letters. That makes you prejudiced against them.'

'I need to know what the students are going through so I can help them.'

In the pause that followed, he thought: Why do you need to know? It's nothing to do with you what other people are going through.

'Send them to Aramani,' he instructed. 'They aren't your responsibility.' And yet behind this moment of seniority, he pictured himself trying to decipher a letter whose words he couldn't read.

Then: 'You're very sweet, Kasper.'

'Sweet!'

The word infuriated him so much that he had a sudden urge to leap out of the window, escape into the fresh air, be on his own, fill his body with clear water and his mind with silence. But just as he was about to get up, she held him back, laughed, stretched out her hand and stroked his cheek.

Confusion made him rash; out it came in another fawning rush. He was the postmaster. He was responsible for delivering the letters; it was also he who decided which were important enough to be read by Gayan.

'So you don't deliver them all?'

'Not all of them, no.'

'What right have you to decide which should be delivered? Why should I give you letters from my students if you aren't going to pass them on?'

She was right. Why didn't he deliver all the letters? The excuse he made came from the authority of his illiteracy. It was also a lie.

'Gayan reads the serious letters. The rest Viraj deals with.'

'All?'

When so many sat unopened under his bed because he could make no sense of them.

The third morning.

Candlelight and silence.

Beside her again in the chair by the window.

'Do you understand?' he said after a few minutes. 'It's because I trust you that I've told you about the letters.'

'I'll never betray you, Kasper. I love you.' Here her mouth twisted; she was laughing at him.

Lust surged through him. To feel her close and get rid of her at the same time he grabbed her hand. 'You must never use the word love. I am a brother. You're a sister. Don't break your promise.'

But he didn't let go of her hand.

On the plane home, all he could think about was her hand

in his and her words of love, so that the journey up the mountain was a climb not just for the driver but his heart.

Still, Aramani had her own way of exerting power. Walking back through the wide, black gates, Amba was there to greet him, spittle at the corners of his mouth as he jabbered on about having seen another tiger, how he had missed Kasper, how Banhi had fallen off her chair during a meditation class because she'd been asleep.

'Gayan has announced a special meal for tonight so there'll be double portions for you, Kasper.'

And with the relief of family and belonging, he went into the large meditation room to one side of the courtyard as if it were easier to greet the picture of Gayan than the man in person. Then there was the swing with its double seat on which he sometimes lay watching the stars when he couldn't sleep.

So Aramani returned to him as a being afresh, untrammelled by sorrow, for the silence observed was like the in-and-out pull of the tide which, in its ebb, took all darkness away. This beautiful place where they were all on the same path, even if at different points and in different moods. Something vast and expansive canopied them yet kept them free and distinct. And there were so many of them but so little noise and no one enquired about anything too closely and it was easy to hide. So that slowly the days which followed took up their rhythm once more.

How hard he worked for the next four months. Day and night, like someone tussling with a minuscule knot, he laboured to break the tie with this woman who had touched his cheek and told him of her love. Picture after picture he drew, evening after evening he pounded round the lake, ran up and down Jagar Rock, rose an hour earlier

135

than usual, until his body hurt more than she hurt inside
him. And he was safe.

28

A few months on.

Monsoon season.

Late morning.

The rain pounding down. Everyone in Macs and boots, slopping through the puddles, each with his own way of keeping warm, of stopping small personal possessions from moulding and spirits from lowering. Paint peeling from the walls, everywhere the smell of damp. The warm centre of Aramani, its courtyard, where the residents sat in the sun after work, where he and Amba had met when he was a child, where day after day Viraj read the newspaper, where the Westerners gossiped, was now a cold place they ran across to reach the next spot indoors.

Sloshing to the post room. A stone in his boot. Pulling the boot off, pouring out muddy water, the stone rolling across the floor. Nothing occupying his mind but how to warm up his feet.

Then, as it was always going to, for if there was a canopy over Aramani it was as thin as the veil that hung from Gayan's door, a letter from Amsterdam. And, Hanneke's handwriting before him, he was furious to find himself back by her side in the chair overlooking Prinsengracht.

Wanting to silence his mind before reading, he went straight to his room, slammed the package down on his desk and waited. But his heart had its own life and in seconds he had ripped the envelope open. Inside was a bundle of letters tied with a yellow ribbon.

But no enclosure. No note of explanation. No request.

He was desperately disappointed. Why? What had he expected? A love letter? Yes, for months he had longed for it: the attention of a letter not to someone else, not about a problem and not indecipherable but a personal declaration of love.

And only to him.

Instead, there was a confession to Gayan in which Hanneke told of her relationship with Henry and how she had continued to see him, and that a week earlier she had slept with him in her flat.

Just able to make out these words, Kasper felt as if a floor of the building he had constructed inside himself had suddenly collapsed leaving only rubble and dust. For her having told him he loved her and he having pictured the telling more times than he realised, he had come to think of her flat as his own, and now she was confessing to secrets spoken there that had nothing to do with him.

> ...*That night I realised that I love Henry and always have...*

As soon as he put the letter down, all energy drained from his body and he was forced to face the fact that it was the memory of her words of love, as much as his own spiritual efforts, that had been the momentum behind his ascent during these last few months. So, as always, when mental storms blew up, he moved from desk to bed, where he lay for two hours, strenuously guiding his thoughts back to safety.

At the precise moment when he found his peace, that place of fact where perspective is restored, he registered a tug on his consciousness – a truth. And the truth was this: whatever her words, his connection with Hanneke was at the start not the end of its life.

29

It was late afternoon. Thinking back on all this about Hanneke had made Kasper restless. He left his room and strode up the hill into the courtyard where he saw a free chair. Five minutes passed. Several people he recognised walked by.

Hot tears filled his eyes. Slowly he stood up, as if only movement could push them away, and for the first time since his return, he allowed himself to visit the milk room.

Aramani's kitchens were poky and dark. As a child, this had been part of their charm for, if the glare of the courtyard buffed the soul to a shine, in the darkness he could relax and be held.

The milk room had the dimness of a stable at night; it was also well-organised and clean like an old-fashioned sweetshop full of jars and pots and packages, and the twins who worked there were so solid and strong that they had both earthed and consoled him.

Kasper realised that he had been rationing himself since his return. He had resisted the milk room because he was afraid of the warmth with which the twins might greet him and the guilt that warmth would compound in him.

However far away, everyone comes back in the end.

As he moved along the narrow open corridor fretted with doorways, he let the scene create itself ahead of him: Anil and Puki slapping him on the back, pulling up his chair, making him a cup of milk, asking him about England, London, the trains, the cricket, whether he had had a good time in Europe, as if it had only been a routine absence that had taken him from Aramani.

On his way, he passed the infirmary. An elderly brother was seated, head tilted back, mouth open, a small wooden spatula pressed against his tongue. The nurse spoke a few words, then handed him a vial of white pills that looked like small sweets. The old brother laughed, and Kasper remembered how he, too, had found such a vial of small sweets had freed him of sorrow – unless the brother was laughing at his remedy?

If so, another innocence spoilt.

You need sorrow to understand night.

Perhaps, in denial of this newly-acquired truth, evasion was what he had hoped for; that once in the milk room all doubts would disperse and he'd be back with the sense that finally he had come home.

But when he opened the door, the milk room was empty: nothing on the shelves, no vats of milk, no twins.

'Where are they?' he asked the first person he saw. 'Where are Puki and Anil?'

'Left,' said a brother carrying a tray of sweets from the main kitchen.

'Why?'

141

'Thrown out.'

Thrown out?

No one was ever *thrown out* of Aramani. Westerners went home but, as far as he knew, he was the only resident who had ever left, and he hadn't been thrown out.

'Why?'

'No idea.'

'What about the chai? Who boils the milk for the chai?'

His back turned, the brother laughed. 'Chai? We've been using teabags for years. Except on Wednesdays.'

Teabags! He might as well have said the words pork or bottom or bikini. But Kasper was also disturbed because he needed to shout his question. Once, people had come up close to him, looked into his eyes then whispered their worries. Now, eliciting information was such a struggle that he felt like a beggar.

Beggar, child, doubter. Too many feelings. Everything unclear. Even his clothes, newly made as Anouka had instructed and returned to him by the same dhobi as the Elders used, didn't look quite clean. And the mix up had its own weary force so that instead of walking away he kept moving into the darkness. Back past the infirmary, across the courtyard, out of the gates and up the path opposite Aramani's entrance to where he had seen the two domes of that vast new building on his first day back. In his mind, they seemed now to have something to do with the teabags, the loss of the twins and what was all wrong with this new Aramani.

As he approached the first building, he saw it was surrounded by a black fence and above its front gate, the name: The White Light Guest House. He peered through the fence railings at the manicured gardens, beside them a swimming pool and wooden loungers. A young woman lay reading. He thought he had seen her before. And was this where Balvan and Mina were now staying? Would they too emerge in a moment to bare their flesh to the Aramani sun?

His retreat was sudden and fast. Back down the hill to the courtyard. That was the same. But teabags, bright light hotels! He was furious. Next, as if he had to see everything and at the same time nothing more, he went to the post room just inside the main gates.

No change.

The same chair he had sat on to sort out the letters, the blue lino-covered table with sheets of paper, envelopes and pens which residents used to write notes, the labelled pigeonholes, his own name still there beside Gayan's... He sat down, then lowered his head to the table. For every mistake he had ever made seemed to have had its beginning in this small, simple room.

30

Three weeks after the arrival of Hanneke's first package in which she had written to Gayan of her relationship with Henry, another turned up. He took it outside, walked along the road away from Aramani, in the direction of Yanna Lake then up towards Jagar Rock.

As he began climbing, he heard a brother who worked in the kitchen shouting, 'Be careful, Kasper, don't fall!' As with all words in those days, he took their warning metaphorically when all that was meant was that the wind was high and his tall, slim body in its flimsy clothing might be blown over.

He hated his hands as they fumbled in the cold, snatching at the envelopes to stop them from flying away. Finally, he managed to lodge them under a stone, except for one that, slipping out from between the others, was addressed not to Gayan but to him. The letter he had always longed to receive.

But not saying this, not these horrible words:

> *Dear Kasper*
> *I'm giving up The Philosophy…*

When he had read on as far as he was able, he lay for over two hours, watching the sun as it slipped down then performed its small silent click and disappeared behind the line of the horizon.

The cold that was also his fear moved through his body until he was unable to get up. The letter, which went on to describe, in such simple terms that he could understand them, Hanneke's reasons for abandoning The Philosophy, expressed everything he realised had been going on in himself: he too had come to dislike the coercive language that she criticised, he too loved art, and, above all, was attracted as she was to beauty, whether of man, woman or object.

He knew he should return to his room, but something had broken inside him so that the tension of his tight hold on life had involuntarily loosened and he could make himself do nothing.

Had he turned around, he would have seen the lights on Yanna Lake. But he wanted to face neither lake nor light. Just to stare at the horizon, the frontier with Pakistan, his own fate...

He started to think things he hadn't even imagined before – about how it might feel to tumble over the edge of the rock, let go and fall. He also thought about sex. What little he knew he considered quite rationally, and realised that somewhere along a line he never knew he had been walking, he had lost the notion of it being a sin; it was just a sensation which, but for the cold, he would have allowed himself here in the open.

Then his thoughts turned to his mother and what she had looked like when she was dead: her face, body, her clothes, and whether in the final hours of her life, his father had been with her. More than all this, he felt the fact of her simply not existing.

Things fade when the sun comes up, and when it did and he was still on the rock, he told himself he'd had the equivalent of a dream whose power would lose its grip when he returned to Aramani and walked into day. All that had happened was he'd read a letter saying that Hanneke was leaving. So what? He was still here, still safe in his lift and his routine.

Everything the same.

Except himself.

For if you spend a night outside Aramani, you change. Because you create a memory. And whatever The Philosophy said about the past being behind you, memories can never be erased as by magic.

Again and again, he thought about her and whether or not he should try and write to her. Not that her letter invited a response or one that he had the skill to word. She had made her decision and he had only to do his duty and pass on what she'd written to Gayan. But he didn't do his duty because in the course of her second letter, she had mentioned her first which was with all the other letters from Amsterdam that he hadn't delivered. He also convinced himself that if Gayan came to know of her decision, she would never be able to leave quietly; she'd be summoned and questioned, given gifts to persuade her to stay. Although Gayan found the foreigners' questions a nuisance, he needed to keep them in order to convince others that The Philosophy wasn't just a refuge for those unable to survive in the world but a truth the world itself lacked.

The greatest effort Kasper made in the weeks that followed his night on Jagar Rock had nothing to do with practising silence or getting up early and everything to do with not writing to Hanneke. But as it turned out they were wasted efforts for a few months later she appeared in Aramani of her own accord.

31

Still seated in the post room, Kasper took a last glance at the pigeonholes as if committing the name of each resident to memory. Only an hour remained before he was due back in the lift. Had he been in Amsterdam or London, he might have taken a shower, wandered the streets, visited an art gallery or the café; made an attempt, at least, to counteract the ache.

Here there was nothing.

Even the mountain paths were imprinted with Aramani, as were the villagers whose shop owners used slogans from The Philosophy to attract custom.

So he started moving slowly in the direction of the lift, head lowered to avoid communication. It was wrong what they said about people seeing the soul not the body. Since his return it was his body and face they seemed to scrutinise, as if he had changed into a stranger.

'Slow, slow, slow,' were the words he spoke under his breath, reverting by reflex to a game he had played as a small child when his parents had taken him on car journeys and he had stared out of the window at the lines on the road. 'Long one, long one, long one.' As the length of the lines changed he'd start up again: 'Short one, short one, short one.' When all lines stopped, he would shout in terrified jubilation: 'None, none, no lines!' Not knowing what he was referring to in those long-ago years when his parents had loved him, they had laughed.

By the time he reached the teaching block, he was weary at the prospect of spending another four hours in the lift. And, as if someone had heard him, he saw as he approached two strips of yellow tape criss-crossed against the lift door and a notice announcing its closure. At this, he was even more upset than he had been by the hotel or the memories provoked by the post room, so that suddenly his feet were on the move, running, dashing, flying to Anouka.

'What's happened?'

'Happened?'

'To the lift.'

'Broken.'

'Why?'

'No idea.' The lack of personal pronoun, so strange in her voice, came out like a snub.

'How long will it take to mend?'

'The lift has been broken for a long time.'

Whatever was actually meant by these words, in his own terms, Kasper knew she was right. The lift had lost its power the day Hanneke had returned to Aramani.

It was four months after he had read her letter on Jagar Rock. He was sitting in the lift drawing when the light suddenly flashed. He pressed the button to open the door and there…

The girl-boy that was Hanneke. Blonde hair cropped even shorter than before, eyes blue-cold and intense, telling him to keep the lift moving, she wanted to talk to him, she knew he wouldn't deliver her letter to Gayan, that she hadn't come back to join Aramani but to fetch him.

Immediately the veil came down, her words not reaching him; only her slim white-clad body so close to his, her softly accented voice so certain...

'Why are you closing your eyes? You need to listen. Kasper, you're special, precious, you need to hear this. You're the only link there is between East and West.'

But he couldn't *hear this*. He could only feel her presence. Stretching out his arm his hand touched her shoulder. Then he remembered Amba's story of the blind men each trying to identify an elephant by different means. But this was less focused. More like sleep, dreaming, a new fragrance, an intuition, a signal, the devil, everything mixed together, both terribly clear and faint as a whisper. On and on and on, as they hung in mid-air and she kept talking.

Of how, she went on, he'd outgrown Aramani, had learnt all that could be learnt here, he should see the world, *the outside world,* which needed his wisdom, *there are wars raging,* Kasper, *political disasters, blunders.*

He told her he'd never heard of the word blunder.

'Don't worry about words. What the world need is your silence.'

Then how she'd booked seats already. The bus from Yanna for two days later, that Aramani must have his passport because if they didn't he wouldn't have been able to fly to Amsterdam the first time. As for a plane ticket, that could be bought in Ahmedabad; she would pay.

And suddenly, like a person finding something they never knew they'd lost, her words pierced the veil and he saw she was right. He *had* outgrown Aramani. The speed of his knowing was as fast as all intuitions, and as disarming. Still, when he opened his eyes, he deflected her, gabbled on about nothing, her life, how she was. As if conversing underwater, he heard her explain that she still lived in the same flat in Amsterdam, but no longer went to the studio. Her time was spent painting, reading and writing articles for an Arts magazine. She meditated on her own and felt she was preparing for something, although she wasn't sure what.

He remembered the early morning silence in her flat a year earlier, the sense that he, too, had a destiny to fulfil but like her wasn't sure what it was. Then again, her impressing it upon him that he was needed, blessed, gifted, he must come immediately, donate to the world what he'd learnt, as if he were a messiah or prophet.

At this, his ego inflated to the size of the globe he was about to travel. And the image of his soul as a flying bird returned to him and he thought: so that's what was meant by The Philosophy. One should be a flying bird, migrate to the West and create a new flock.

Now, as he thought about it, he recalled how this image of himself had already begun forming in his mind long before Hanneke had returned, of how he had known deep down that living a spiritual life couldn't only involve sitting all day in a lift.

Still, he was terrified. Again and again they'd been warned that those who imagined they could form breakaway groups would suffer severe punishment not from Gayan but from life itself.

But on and on she had gone with her reasons and impositions.

'It will give you more scope to draw, too. We're both artists. Artists need freedom. You can't draw the same thing over and over. You need to have new experiences.'

She was right. After all, for his whole time in Aramani, hadn't he lived more as an artist than a follower; as a child, free to draw and wander; as a young adult, as ambitious as a protégé learning to paint from a master? It was true he'd enjoyed a few years of conformity, when his attention to The Philosophy had matched the attention he paid to himself. But he had always been governed by independence, pursuing his own interests: sketching, doodling, writing single letters over and over in a vague attempt to become literate – that last, never with much zest. He'd also given classes which were inspired and off-course so that he was aware if he carried on in the same vein he'd cause chaos.

He knew all this without knowing he knew. But she knew. And so the other truth was that, as soon as she invited him to join her, his life in Aramani was over.

32

All this, Kasper tried to assess in the measured fashion The Philosophy so encouraged. But he kept getting muddled. In all his time in Aramani he had never once learnt anything when his mood had been troubled whereas he saw now that in the outside world he had only ever understood a significant truth when he'd been upset.

The lift. Hanneke had been right about that. What value was there in a lift? People should use the stairs. Yet the manageable space of the lift permeated every cell of his being. Even when he'd left, he had returned to the lift in his mind.

And now it was gone.

The last thing gone.

Heart aching, he returned to Anouka and asked her again when it would be mended. She told him to go away, she was busy, and anyway, once the lift had been renovated it would be automated so he wouldn't be needed any more.

Whatever the truth, they always win in the end.

That evening, Kasper ate as usual with the Elders, then wandered down the road to Yanna Lake, his mind so preoccupied that he didn't notice Raj, his childhood enemy, dressed in jeans and T-shirt taking money for boat rides.

I must leave this place soon.

These were the words that came to him as he walked. And, with them, another burst of anger: *You can never leave. The Philosophy is with you forever. Either The Philosophy or darkness.* The lessons go on, but they have no logic, no sequence, and there's no one to say sorry to; if you find love it goes wrong because all you remember is what Aramani has told you – that human love is cursed.

The evening before he ran away with Hanneke, Kasper sat in his room and urgently meditated. But urgency had never brought clarity. Still, he felt it important to make some attempt at communication. So he spoke his statement out loud. 'Gayan, Viraj, Anouka, if you don't want me to go, do something to stop me.'

What had he expected? Some magical warning or sign? An object crashing to the ground, a summons? Words spoken to stop him?

Nothing.

Only one thought occurred to him. The letters. He must do something with the letters he had never delivered.

But who to give them to? Who in Aramani to entrust with such outcries of pain which he had brutally ignored for so long?

Because I can't read. That's why he gave them to me. I can't read and so it was his way of ignoring them.

But knowing this was in some part an excuse, it was his legs that had provided the answer, pelting him into the courtyard, down the hill past Amba's darkroom, the carpenter's workshop, the transport department, out of the back gate, past the camp, up the steps and down into the village.

The bangle-seller. That's who he would give them to.

Why him he had no idea, other than that he had stolen from him in the past and entrusting him with something important felt like repayment.

Back in his room, he felt better, as if he had freed himself of a burden that made packing much easier. He buoyed himself up further on the superstition that because the dhobi had returned his laundry the same afternoon, it must mean it was right to leave.

In slow motion, he lined up five sets of kurtas, two jumpers, a shawl, underwear, socks, two new notebooks, two pens, and a collection of small toiletries. He also packed the brown leather shoes that Anouka had given him.

At ten in the evening he took his case to the room where he'd had his first lessons with Amba, and where he'd hidden the gold robe and crown he'd been forced to wear on the evening of Holi.

Before dawn he left his room, retrieved the case, and walked once more to the village. Pausing beside the water pump, he stared up at the early morning sky and the last of the stars and had the child's sense that they belonged only to Aramani. The farewell to nature slowed his step so that he had to force himself forwards to the marketplace

155

where Hanneke stood waiting.

In the road animals dawdled: dogs, cats, the village donkey… As he and Hanneke greeted each other then waited for the bus, a car swerved round the corner and knocked over a pig. It squealed, rolled on to its back, and seconds later, lay with its stomach open, guts spilt and steaming on the road.

In a rare incidence either of vulnerability or performance, Hanneke shrieked and grabbed his arm, and it was the feel of her weight against him that kept him going. For if the clean laundry was a good omen, the squealing pig, like some part of himself crying out, was a bad one.

It was at the airport that Kasper felt his departure from Aramani most keenly. On the few journeys he'd ever taken, he had trained himself not to look at strangers. Now, he didn't know if he was free of the rule of averting his eyes or was still living by The Philosophy. Either way, he stared. Every woman, man, child, he allowed entry into the high room inside him.

And away from Aramani, not dressed in white, who was this Hanneke, he wondered? A sister, lover, enemy? He had never been so confused about anyone, because to this point, he had related to all Westerners from a position of superiority.

Now he felt himself slipping and falling.

At least silence was still an ally; a state long nurtured and, for the moment at least, invulnerable to the quick influx of new impressions.

For years Kasper had been surrounded by such a rich

mix of fragrances that in some ways he had lived more like an animal than a human, sniffing out the next safe place in which to hide: breathing in the bright mountain air, fingering the gauzy delicacy of fabrics – soft, light, billowing – as residents swung shawls loosely about their shoulders and in mid-winter pulled down over their heads white woollen headscarves and hats, like skiers in the chill.

Now, in the course of a day's flight, home contracted into a three-roomed flat where life was lived almost constantly inside. There were no moves to be made from steps to lift to door to room; no mountains, no paths or wild animals; no privacy and no chance to sanctify or compose the atmosphere of this new space.

Like a fretful child, Kasper felt as if he had been spun blindfold in circles and landed in a box barely bigger than the lift he had abandoned. Worry made his head light; he knew he must find something to fix on. First food became the focus, then the bathroom, what time he would get up, go to bed; the shape of the day and the night.

Hanneke did all she could to help, telling him to eat what and when he liked, to take his time, relax, sleep, go out, stay in… And that was even more confusing because he needed to be told and yet to be free, and you couldn't have both.

For the first hour of that first night in Amsterdam, fear of what he had done assaulted him in a series of shocks that sent that familiar but always new pain balling into his lower back. He lay flat, sat up, stood, walked to the window, stared at the bicycles locked for the night, the boats on the canal with its dark, brackish water; heard once more the bells of Westerkerk, then forced himself to return to the divan on which he had slept during his first stay. Finally, he fell into a light doze.

Early the next morning, he heard a man shouting and, still drowsy, his mind was transported back to Delhi, the day his mother had left for England, when far beneath their shared room someone had called to a resident to boil water for tea.

On waking, Hanneke came and sat on his bed, told him she had a few spare hours before returning to work and that it would be useful for him to see a little of the city.

'Why?'

'Because you need to meet the world as it is.'

33

During those first days in Amsterdam, the shock of arrival and all the anxieties it provoked suppressed any sense of what he and Hanneke meant to each other. In the end, Kasper began to think of her as a sister or brother in whose company he might climb even higher than he had in Aramani. For cramped as it was, at least he was free of the rush and clatter of India.

In fact, it was with a kind of immoral speed that he conducted the first casting off of Aramani, as if Amba, old Bahni, Anouka, Viraj, and most serious of all, Gayan, no longer existed. But just as he was floating free in this strange daze of peace, Hanneke struck a new, unwelcome note, insisting once more that they go out. This time, he knew he had to say yes, and that acceptance was the beginning of a new phase which would involve compromise, a word he disliked for its softness.

'You'll need a coat,' she said, passing him a man's Mac. 'And it's time we got you some new clothes.'

'I've already got shoes.' And he pointed to the brogues Anouka had given him, wondering if the old woman had known they didn't belong in Aramani any more than he did?

'You can't walk round in pyjamas and brogues, Kasper.'

'Brogues?'

'Those!'

'Why not?'

He heard the stupidity of his words as he spoke them and knew she was right. But he was angered by the sense that something important was being taken from him.

'And let's get your hair styled properly.'

'Why?'

Her answer was a mere gesture of her hands as if it were obvious that there was something strange about his appearance.

Once in the streets, commotion and repetition disconcerted him. Everywhere seemed the same: canals, cars, bicycles, the babble of people talking a language he didn't understand. There was no caste system here, no way of knowing what background anyone was from; whether educated or not, good or not, cultured, ignorant... He tried to think it didn't matter, reminding himself for the thousandth time that the whole point of The Philosophy was that all people were equal. But he knew it wasn't true. Even in Aramani, particularly in Aramani in fact, residents were ranked.

They walked for ten minutes or so, Hanneke pointing on the way to a café, telling him that the man who ran it would make a good friend. 'His name's Lars. He's a great guy.' At this, Kasper was offended. He hadn't come here to visit cafés, to meet *great guys*. Surely there was more to it than that! She ignored his protest, pointing up at the shopping centre.

'It used to be Holland's biggest post office! Just the right place for you, Kasper.' To this quip he gave no response for he was thinking the same and the same brought a thousand anxieties.

They spent what felt like hours in this monstrous place of acquisition. Encountering escalators for the first time, they went up and down, in and out of shops that looked thrown together like renovated market stalls all under a single roof. Hanneke knew exactly where she was going, and within minutes had chosen at least five outfits for him to try on. This was how they did things in India: bought in bulk although there, they bought five of the same item whereas here Hanneke chose a variety: jeans, shirts, a jacket, more shoes...

By the end Kasper was irritable.

'But you look fantastic!'

He disliked the word fantastic and objected, in particular, to jeans. An item of clothing coveted by many young Indians, he found them uncomfortable.

At the hair salon, the stylist took one look, spoke a few words to Hanneke, led him to a basin, guided his head back into the cup of his hands and attempted a head massage. Here, in a loss and gain process that lasted the length of his time in Amsterdam, Kasper recovered some sense of a self that he recognised. For if he knew nothing about fashion, he knew about head massage. Discovering this, the stylist tempered his tone, but not as far as to take his customer's wishes into account.

'That's better.'

As if he needed mending! And with this thought he was overcome by a desire for paper. Earlier they had passed a shop selling brushes and paint; he had longed to stop and look, but there was the problem of money.

'What's wrong?'

Everything was wrong. For while he was attracted to Hanneke and admired her assurance, he felt resentful that she wished to change him, when it had been he who had had it in mind to change her.

34

On a day set in advance, as if to mark a moment of importance, they moved a small table to the window, positioned notebook and pens, water, a clock and sat for ten minutes in silence, after which she blurted out the question that pressed her.

'Do you have to die to become a Traveller?'

Never talk to the foreigners about The Travellers. Tell them that if they want that kind of thing, they should visit a fortune-teller.

But no fortune-teller could speak to them about The Travellers. And nor was he going to speak about them. Not here, outside India.

When she pushed him, he raised his hand. And the refusal seemed to please her as much as his agreement to live with her, because it set a boundary and the boundary sprung open another door in his mind, as if the room inside him led to a higher room still, that was small and utterly private.

The meditation that evening was their first serious attempt at creating a shared version of what Aramani taught. And the act was one forged as much out of intimacy as spirit, the very two qualities which to this point had been kept so forcefully apart, except with Gayan who had always hugged him so freely.

And Amba…

Yet something served their courage. For after twenty minutes in silence, the light of the teaching room, and later the temple, began shining here too.

When it was she who spoke first, asking if he'd seen it as she had, Kasper was filled with relief, because the light was confirmation that, in living with Hanneke, he wasn't sacrificing all he had built in Aramani; he was here for a reason. What that reason was, he still didn't know, other than that they were pioneers, above the rules, yet important. And being important was all that had mattered to him then.

35

It was saddening to recall all this about Hanneke and Holland and the ill-conceived roles they had imagined for themselves. Now there was no drama. Just the present: rice, dhal, chapattis, and the quiet concentration of the Elders as they made a tent of their fingers and chewed.

But Aramani hadn't entirely lost its capacity to surprise. First, the new hotel with its swimming pool then the closure of the lift. And now, in the dining room for supper, an unexpected array of delicacies in small silver dishes and amid them, a dignitary with long face and hefty appetite.

On his right sat Viraj, on the other, a beautiful young resident whom Kasper had never seen before. Looking at her closely, it struck him that, in her refinement, the act of eating itself seemed somehow an affront to her beauty. Still, when she gestured to the empty seat on her left, Kasper joined her, irritated that it was only in the presence of important outsiders that men and women were permitted to dine side by side.

Behind him, Kala watched as Kasper downed his food fast. He knew what she was thinking. From the start, she had disapproved of him swanning around Aramani as if he owned the place. She wanted him away and yet wanted him there too, if only for a while, as that precious link between West and East that Hanneke had talked so much about. And indeed, as he rose to leave, she pounced on him, informing him that a group of Americans were visiting and she'd like him to give them a talk on ethics in business.

'In the new auditorium.'

'I've not been in there and anyway I don't know anything about ethics in business.'

'What does that matter? You'll make an excellent job of it. I'll speak a few words at the beginning, then you'll give the main speech. First you can talk about Europe and then tell them about Aramani.'

In his room Kasper seethed. How he detested this side of Aramani! The way it chivvied and grabbed at people: politicians, film stars, businessmen, charming them with good food and gifts and a few moments of peace, in an attempt to convince them that there was only one way of seeing the world, and that heaven wasn't waiting for them in another dimension or an undiscovered spot on earth, but was here in India, only India.

And to think: I believed all that myself.

And what, too, if he did speak about his time in Europe – his intimacy with Hanneke, Lars, his having consumed alcohol? Perhaps this was his chance to enact a grown-up equivalent of the sin of graffiti he'd been guilty of as a child – a defacement of Aramani with his own vivid mix of colours?

He was shocked by this intention because it felt so close to being realised when ten years earlier he would have died for The Philosophy.

Standing on the narrow ledge outside his room, he looked out at the darkening line of the mountains. A small light darted at speed: two boys on a bicycle, the older skimming his foot fast over the bumps, his friend in front of him, holding a torch. When they reached a dip in the slope, the torch went out. Five minutes later, the light began moving again.

Half a dozen times they went up and down. On one descent, the smaller boy must have dropped the torch. There was a scramble to find it. The bicycle rolled away; the bigger boy ran after it. Then there was laughter and screeching. Finally, silence. Kasper peered over his balcony railings in search of them but could see nothing. He only heard words loud in his head.

The Light has gone out.

36

A month after the clothes-buying trip in Amsterdam, Kasper felt such an urgency to begin drawing again that he asked Hanneke to bring him paper from her workplace. She agreed as easily as if passing him a glass of water, having no idea how much that water was needed to keep him alive.

When, rough-textured and thick, the sketchpad arrived in two perfect white blocks, he began with a drawing of the two chairs by the window, then the clock, the divan where he slept, its pillows and quilt. After that, he walked to the window and tried drawing a bicycle.

A week later, sufficiently restored by these small acts of creation to ask for some money, he left the flat for the first time alone, beginning what was to become one of his greatest pleasures while in Amsterdam: its art. His tastes were formed fast. Renoir, he admired because of the way he used light, but it was Van Gogh he loved more. And after a time, he began visiting his museum regularly.

Again and again he stood before the same pictures: the little post boy in the cap who reminded him of himself, the Old Woman's Head, a painting he liked because the shape of the face was so like old Banhi's.

'You don't approve,' he said out loud as he

approached her one day. 'You think I've made a mistake leaving Aramani.'

Her face didn't change because her face wasn't Banhi's.

When he came to the thick, caked oils the artist had used in Saint-Rémy, he had to force himself to look for fear that, being in their presence too long, he would fall into the same sorrow himself.

It was the first time Kasper fully understood Aramani's assertion that there was nothing wrong with the act of creation, it was where the creation took you that was dangerous, for as much as he loved art, there were times when he left his trips to the galleries feeling sad.

Apart from these, Kasper made himself at home in the café that Hanneke had pointed out to him on their way to the shopping centre, because it was close to the flat and the dark wood, cushion-less benches and peeling paint reminded him a little of the studio in Delhi that he had stayed in with his mother prior to her departure for London.

The owner, Lars, a quiet man some ten years older than Kasper, didn't mind him sitting for stretches of time, buying so little. In fact, after a few weeks, he told him he could come to the café just to draw.

It was Lars who introduced him to black coffee which sometimes, when the café closed for an hour, they drank side by side. It was here, too, away from Hanneke's judging eyes, that Kasper practised reading from English magazines that Lars kept in a pile at the end of the counter.

'Read something out,' Lars said one day. 'It will help you.'

Kasper felt cornered.

'How did you know about my reading?'

'Because you mouth the words and you point at the line.'

In reply, Kasper withdrew into himself, took out his sketchpad and drew Lars as he dried cups and saucers on an old tea towel.

Three months into his stay, Kasper ventured out further. Tramping from street to street he remembered how, once, Gayan had cupped his face and said, 'Kasper, always stay in the gathering or one day you'll get lost.' He tried to block out this memory, telling himself that he *was* in a crowd, a gathering. Amsterdam was always full, after all: people queuing, dawdling, snapping pictures. But they weren't *his people;* that's what Gayan meant.

And one day he did get lost. Hour after hour he wandered around, endlessly meeting the same street name.

If you get lost, ask an Elder. Always ask an Elder.

But there was no Elder. And the fact of his need for one combined with the weakness of his own head infuriated him. Amsterdam wasn't his place, wasn't his home; it would always be a mystery as everywhere except Aramani was a mystery.

That evening Hanneke returned late from work. Kasper thought she looked different although he knew it might be he who had changed. Wearing a white, silk kimono, she went to take a shower, saying she didn't feel like eating, she'd just have a glass of green tea.

Later, perhaps feeling bad that she'd ignored him, she stretched out her hand and drew him to where she was sitting on the floor beneath the window.

And out of the dusk, she repeated the words she had spoken during his first stay.

'I love you, Kasper. As a woman loves a man.'

And her voice carried no irony. If anything, it was muted, so that instead of wondering why this moment of confusion was the right one to begin their physical life together, with shaking hands he held the round smoothness of her head and kissed her.

Eleven the same evening.

For the first time, she showed him her room and her body. Like an artist taking notes, he sat on her bed and stared: the square shoulders, the small curve where they met her upper arms, the modest round of her breasts... And the more he looked, the more he wanted to look and at the same time turn away.

'I want to see your back.'

And there she was, buttocks strong, torso wide and straight. At a loss, he closed his eyes.

'I need to be alone now.'

She laughed.

'No. It's your turn, Kasper. I'll help you.'

The rigmarole of undressing compounded his confusion – the undoing of buttons, arms out of sleeves as if he were a girl and she the seducer. Then she was like the teacher in his childhood dream, throwing out kurtas to the class and everyone changing back into their uniform.

Seeing his shame, she took the white kimono from her chair and placed it around him.

'Keep it. It suits you.'

That night they slept side by side for the first time. And through his sleep, his body moved in a rhythm which shamed him. He kept waking himself up and looking at everything in the room, as if to pull the walls towards him: the pictures of the sea, the grey and cream dressing table with its bottles and creams lined up like small pots of paint, black dresses strewn over a chair.

He wanted to draw her clothes, the light above the bed with the crystal shades on the end of each of its curved arms, the bookcase… As if the act of reproducing objects on paper would rescue him from the speed of change she was forcing upon him.

After a few hours, he woke, and there she still was. Guiltily he leant over, duvet thrown back, and studied her sleeping body.

'Now?'

The panic was acute. He wanted to hide, run away, sleep on his own. But she took her time.

'Kasper, tell me more about The Travellers.'

And as if reference to this private aspect of The Philosophy both excused yet intensified the intimacy between them, he finally succumbed, lying back and explaining how those who studied The Philosophy deeply, and then died, were said to be re-born into families that would be protected from the turbulence of the world's final moments. She laughed, saying she knew that was what The Philosophy said, but what about children who were born of brothers and sisters still in their current life? And in the private room in his mind that was still a place of self-glorification and exceptions, he realised that he, too, had been entertaining the idea that if he and Hanneke ever had a child, it might be a Traveller Child.

That night, the first of their intimate life together, he found the idea more arousing than the thought of the action that might bring it about. For Aramani taught that a man loses his innocence when he has sex. But now it seemed to Kasper that innocence was exactly what sex restored, for being the only act which made one person fully visible to another. When his climax came, he was more astonished than he had been by the shining of any light. And more worried too, for something about the act had been unappealing, shocking even, as if she, indeed any woman, was the wrong person with whom to have sex.

Afterwards she said, 'Kasper, let's have a child. A Traveller Child.' Whatever he had been thinking before, the sound of these words in her voice was all wrong. They took no account of the love that should surely exist between them first. But it was too late. His body drove him now, so that, against all that his conscience had ever instructed, he wanted only to repeat what he had just done. And do it better.

He hated her going to work the next morning because the second she'd left his mind became vengeful. Guilt, questions, confusion... And a sense that his own life had been wiped out while a new one might even now be in the making and he barely more than a child himself.

So that was what The Philosophy meant.

Surrender to lust and you fall as if from a high building so that your bones are crushed.

While he longed to sit still he forced himself out into the rain. He was weighed down by himself and himself was the rain. And the sky was neither grey nor white but a bruised purple and the purple was also him.

He was standing by the window wearing the kimono when Hanneke returned that evening. No words were exchanged and he felt suddenly that he had wronged her. In a strange moment of admission, she worded his shock for him, explaining that she understood what he must feel and was sorry.

Then they cooked together and ate at the table beside the window. These small actions of making were calming, although what they had done in the night seemed to swim through her easily, leaving neither mark nor disorientation whereas his entire being was shaken.

Again she came back to it.

'Imagine a Traveller Child, Kasper! How carefully we'd have to look after him.'

Only later did he recall her use of the word *him* for a child not, as far as he knew, even conceived *because that's not how you do it, Kasper. You need to learn a lot more about sex. It will take time.*

In a fit of pique, he returned to the café. It was unusually full. People dressed in tight clothing, chattering, laughing and all in voices he couldn't understand.

'A cycling event,' explained Lars.

The words baffled Kasper, transporting him at once to Amba and the temple then London when he was six and had been given a bicycle for Christmas. How his father had taught him to keep his balance. Each lunchtime between the end of December and the middle of January, the man, now a stranger, had walked by his side, his hand on his back until after three weeks Kasper could ride the bike on his own.

At the thought of this man whose face he could barely remember, he felt a sudden wave of guilt. He must write to him, tell him where he was, say something, anything, to show he still cared… He had kept the notebook in which his address was hidden.

To the sound of laughter, drinks being poured, the coffee machine clanking and burbling, he tried to begin.

Dear Father…

Dear Pop

Pop

None of these words felt right and he looked with dismay at the infantile quality of his handwriting. How could he be so old and write only as well as a small child?

In the end, he waited for the cyclists to leave.

'What is it?'

'I need your help.'

'With?'

'I –'

But how could he explain, not only that he couldn't read but he couldn't write either? Lars, this strongly-built figure who was able to deal with so many people at once, could so easily laugh, sell, clear up, would surely think him an idiot. But when Lars put down his towel and came once more to sit with him, Kasper felt the man and his kindness and longed to lie next to him.

Yes him.

Not Hanneke.

Him.

Lie next to him and be held.

So that's what was wrong.

'What do you want me to do?' The words were weighted with warmth.

Kasper tightened. The feel of Lars' arm around his shoulder, the strength, the comfort...

'Could you write a letter for me? If I say the words out loud? Here, on the drawing pad.'

'Sure. What do you want me to write?'

Inhibited, Kasper started and stopped, started and stopped, eventually keeping the letter to a few lines: where he was now living, how he hadn't forgotten his father...

But he knew this was a lie. He *had* forgotten his father. It was only because Lars showed no emotion that he was able to let the man know where he was and ask him if he was well. Of his mother, he wrote nothing.

'I haven't got an envelope by the way.'

Lars shrugged and smiled. Their faces were very close. 'Ask Hanneke.'

Kasper was too relieved that the letter was now written to notice the coldness in Lars' voice.

Back in the flat, Kasper felt an unexpected awkwardness when making his request.

'Who are you writing to anyway?'

'My father.'

'But you've left him behind.'

'I want him to know where I am. So can you put a stamp on my letter and post it?'

Very slowly in capital letters he wrote Surya's name on the envelope, addressed it to London and handed it to her.

'It won't bite you!' Kasper said, wanting to snap her into obedience, this woman who was suddenly so imperious.

'Won't it?'

One day, soon after they had begun sharing a bed, Hanneke returned from work, her arms full. Trained not to pry he usually left her to unpack her bags on her own. But for some reason, which now made him trust life more than any theory of how it worked, his hands made their own decision.

Fruit, vegetables, milk and fresh cheeses from the market; yoghurts, biscuits and a favourite kind of tea they had found in a store near the Rijksmuseum. Then a small, white bag, on it a Dutch brand name. Inside, a package wrapped in tissue paper. This, he opened with care as if, like the tiger he and Amba had seen in the mountains, it might come alive and pounce.

And there it was, unfolded and flat on the top of the bag: an infant's white cardigan.

His body began shaking.

> *You told us to mistrust the body, but looking back it's the only thing that has ever told the truth.*

Perhaps she wanted him to see it because, still in her coat, she rushed at him, laughed, held him. And seeking out the soft curve of her neck, he put it to her: 'Why clothes for a baby?'

No answer.

This angered him for it was the kind of dismissal of which his mother and Anouka were guilty when asked a direct question, as well as so many of the Elders for whom the deflection from question to slogan was a way of maintaining superiority.

'Why don't you just tell me?'

'I'm sorry,' she said. 'I've hinted at it a couple of times but you don't listen.'

'Why hint?' His body fumed. 'What is there to hint about with someone you love?'

At this, she began crying, sobbing, shaking and he pulled her towards him, because whatever her manner of telling, to have a child with her seemed all of a sudden the answer to his own sorrow. But then he said something that surprised him so much it might have been someone else who had spoken. How he was pleased for her. *Not for them, but for her…*

As if he already knew how their story would end.

37

Kasper stood in the wings of the auditorium, a vast space with a stage almost as big as Amsterdam's Westerpark. There was nothing of Aramani about it, other than the white-sheeted floor. Even the pictures of The Philosophy weren't in the normal style but misty and abstract, in fact not unlike the paintings Hanneke was so skilled at. Fast dismissing the thought that they might indeed have been painted by her, commissioned to provide her with an extra income (unless she had donated them for nothing?), he returned to his talk. Just as in the past, when he had relied on inspiration he had done no preparation. But then he had always been calm; now his mind was filled with confusion.

For what to say?

Other than to tell of the events of his past? But which past? His life as a spiritual authority or his experience as a young man increasingly given to questions and yearnings?

As he considered, Kala was already on stage explaining how Aramani had come into being. He was freshly astonished by the force of her voice. Where did it come from? As his ex-wife, did she have special access to Gayan's energy? Could she walk through a door into his mind to the god he claimed to inhabit him? This question somehow made him think of Amsterdam and his body weakened so that, without wanting to, he found himself leaning for support against the force of her voice.

Peering out at her listeners, he was relieved by the sight of the businessmen's feet, those great dark oblongs like small maps of England replicated over and over. Still, his mouth was dry and suddenly he longed to be back within the four walls of the lift.

The lift that was broken.

When Kala had introduced him, he walked to the centre of the stage. The audience waited; his breathing became shallow. Finally, a young brother appeared from the wings. With care, he tilted the microphone so that it was closer to Kasper's mouth. The small movement performed by slim, brown fingers felt so like a caress that Kasper longed to hold on to him, to tell him to stay there while he spoke. Instead, there was only the microphone, an image of himself, stick-thin and tall.

'Gentleman. I have no experience of your world,' he began. 'I'm not the right person to talk about ethics in business. I know nothing about the subject, don't care for it, have no interest in it. What I can tell you about is Aramani and what it has been like for me since leaving it. Like you, I have lived in the West and never while I was there did I come across a place as beautiful as Aramani. The Philosophy – '

From the front row, Kala's body blazed conviction into his words. Then he saw her move to the doorway to guide into the auditorium the young sister who had sat beside him in the dining room the evening before.

Kala spoke with her quietly and he saw her turning to look at the audience then slipping into a seat in the second row, as if between them, they were capable of creating a canopy of light over these heavily moneyed men.

Perhaps over him too?

Because instead of speaking of doubt or confusion, he suddenly began handing them all his favourite places: Yanna Lake, the courtyard, the khejri trees, the different meditation rooms: how long they had been there, what they meant, what could be felt in each place, after which he so lost control that he even began giving *himself* away.

'I've tried leaving but I can't free myself. And in my view that's a good thing. Everyone needs a place they feel is home. Aramani is generous. It lets anyone own it; anyone who wants it can have it for the time of their stay.'

Kala stood up and smiling broadly walked up the steps to one side of the stage.

For another five minutes he continued. Told them to visit each meditation room: the small hut with the cane roof, the octagonal space situated in the teaching block, the white-sheeted room to one side of the courtyard…

'But beneath all this, you must also see the place for what -'

And suddenly the space was filled.

Kala. An inch from his side, snatching the microphone so that his next words were lost.

'I must stop our speaker. As you know, we began late because of technical problems. I would like to thank you for listening. It's true that every building in Aramani is imbued with meaning –'

Imbued! Christ, how he hated her! The way her voice paraded not her soul, if she even had one, but her position of privilege.

When she went on to mention lunch, he raged at the

181

way Elders used food as a means of persuasion. Then his loathing was turned upon the businessmen who, with their socks and coloured shirts, pens and notebooks, would soon be wolfing down their food then lying bloated and snoring on their beds.

'At four o'clock,' she went on, 'we shall be conducting a tour.'

Workshops! Tours! It was his own fault, he realised. It was he who had spoken the eulogy, dull for being only half-true, so like music with the bass line cut out.

Back in the wings, Kasper stood shaking.

A shape moved nearby.

Human but barely so.

With it, a voice. And a smell which gripped Kasper's chest.

Alcohol.

Surely not. Never in Aramani.

'Kasper, thank you for honouring Aramani.'

Gayan!

Whose voice only loved him when he was on the right side of The Philosophy, which was not how he wished to be loved, as a person bravely returning and trying to understand. But then both voice and body disappeared, as if the old man was either copying the god he protected – appearing in the dark and only in brief – or was hiding.

In the foyer, Kasper bumped into Balvan.

'I smelt drink.' His heart was loud in his chest.

'I enjoyed your speech greatly.'

'But I smelt drink!'

'Never mind about that.'

'Never mind? Of course I mind!

'Now speaking of drink, come and have one with us at the hotel. Mina would love to see you. She hasn't been attending any lectures recently.'

'The lift?'

'We've moved to the hotel. It's more relaxed.' And with Balvan's arm round his shoulder, Kasper became numbly acquiescent. They had only been kind to him, this man with his food and drink and his chattering wife.

On a long chair beside the pool, Mina lay stretched out, the strip of skin between sari top and belly button exposed to the sun. She extended her hand and asked how the talk had gone. The directness of the question brought Kasper back to himself.

'Badly. I said things I didn't mean. Then I smelt drink!'

'Drink. Of course. That's what we need. What would you like?'

'Water.'

'Have something stronger. A thimble of brandy, at least.'

Kasper was alarmed. The smell in the wings, his own experiments with alcohol, which at least he hadn't indulged in here, and now Balvan...? Did the man know of the muddle he was in? Whatever he did or didn't know, Kasper's energy became that of a person chucking a sheaf of papers in the air and letting them land wherever they fell.

The lift gone, Gayan distant, he gave in to the easy agreements, as he had in London when he'd decided it didn't matter what he poured down his throat; after all, it was simply a part of his body, not his soul. In the end, he drank much more than a thimbleful and his head swam through the problems before him.

Indifferent to the contrast between Aramani's food and the meal served up by the hotel, the couple tucked in as they drank. He watched their greed and mused how it would be if they were his parents, and this was a resort where he and Hanneke and the baby were holidaying. The ridiculous sequence of images conjured by a troubled spirit, he batted away fast. The couple were strangers and, kind or otherwise, they talked from the surface of themselves.

Before he rose to leave, Balvan patted his arm and said, 'You can visit us in Bombay whenever you wish. I'll give you our address before we leave.'

The moment Kasper walked away, the couple began arguing so that, returning to his room, he decided they were like a pair of grown-up children, a thought which brought him back to himself, how he was also a child and then to that real child suggested by the small white garment in Hanneke's kitchen.

38

The early months of Hanneke's pregnancy brought an unexpected contentment, for it felt to Kasper as if somehow he, too, was being carried and grown anew. And all he had ever longed for were the things they surrounded themselves with then: light, space, the music of Schubert, Haydn, Mozart's piano concertos; sounds he would have grown up with so much more happily than the monotonous songs that blasted through Aramani's Tannoy system.

Sometimes Hanneke had nightmares. The baby was lost, dead, had never been conceived at all. In these moments, he stepped back into his seniority and comforted her at the loss – not of the baby, *but of himself*.

As the months passed, her skin began to glow in the way the faces of Aramani's residents glowed after they had enjoyed a stretch of silence. It made Kasper long to protect her, and in doing so, save himself. But when the swelling of her stomach became visible, he felt the beginnings of fear. To feel more in control, he made sketch after sketch of things that were fixed: the table by the window, the chairs, kitchen utensils and in Café Prins, he watched the elegant movements of Lars as he cleaned and wiped glasses and waited for customers.

In the later months, when Hanneke reduced her working hours, new instincts drove him. He thought about foraging, finding a bigger flat, getting work… Hanneke was dismissive, reminding him that to achieve anything useful he would need not only qualifications but a work permit. The brush with bureaucracy, his lack of formal education, the fact that she had brought him here, perhaps even to steal his power then abandon him, reawakened the fury he had felt when he'd begun studying The Philosophy seriously, and there was always a rule to cut short any flourishing.

So with a reflex of force that had served him all his life, he pushed all doubts aside and thought only of the pregnancy which was also his own burgeoning. And sometimes Lars, the café owner, to whom he went freely, reconnected him not with the high room inside him, but the fact of himself as an artist and lover not of women but of men.

It was a terrible thing then that one day Hanneke snatched back both her growing child and the space of her flat, yelling at him to get out.

'Just three hours. Give me that, at least. You're here too much. Here, doing nothing.'

He stared at her in terror.

'Go on. Three hours. Four.'

Desperately, Kasper rifled through her bag for money, stumbled into the oversized Mac he had worn on that first day when she had bullied him into shopping.

But where to go? Where to take himself? Lars? But what was Lars? Only plaster for a wound; no answer to what had just happened. Lars would console him when Kasper knew that for this short time at least, he must stand on his own, undefended.

He began walking aimlessly, talking out loud to himself, now and then glancing upwards, wishing he could travel not horizontally along shop-lined streets but high into the sky, as his mind had wont to do on those beautiful early mornings in Aramani. He stretched up his arm as if to touch the white-grey air.

'Mind out.'

The reprimand came from a couple trying to pass.

As if he was a statue in the middle of the pavement.

He looked down at his feet, the only part of him that seemed capable of expressing any wisdom.

The soul has moved into my soles.

He spoke the words in step with his stride and laughed. The notion made no sense and yet chimed with the slogans Gayan had so favoured, as if he thought their ring and their rhymes the only way for the residents to learn and remember:

Old is gold.
A Liar is like fire.
Sin makes a din.

Within minutes, he was back inside the post office building with its mishmash of shops. He looked at the escalator, the way its metal ridges were so close-set, like railway tracks narrow enough for a train to keel over, leaving passengers to scramble out of upside-down windows.

Gingerly he set foot on it, allowed himself to be taken up and up. Then jumped like a child over the teeth that marked its meeting with the chalk-coloured marble of the precinct floor. He thought back to the tailors in the village in Aramani, threading their sewing machines, feet moving up and down on pedals that powered them, lengths of cloth cascading to the floor in folds of bright colour, stitches appearing at speed so that kurtas seemed conjured from sea. Here, there was no sound of making.

Six times, he went up and down the escalator, forgetting to change sides so that he kept being shoved by people in a rush to reach shops whose clothes were not made where they were sold but flown in from faraway lands. How empty the place was and yet full of these people with their bags and their small plastic cards that magically turned into money!

On the ground floor he found a small supermarket, wandered in, ending up before a selection of bottles. There was orange, deep red, tawny brown and liquid that looked only like water. He saw Amba in his mind and called to him: 'What colour do I need?' And his hand went to liquid of no colour apart from a fleck of gold, a reflection from the light. The bottle was heavy and important and cost almost as much as he had stolen from Hanneke's purse.

On a bench in Westerpark he unscrewed the top and took a swig. The bitterness pushed him forwards so that the sky was blotted out and all he could see was grass. Orange shapes swirled in the wind and his head also swirled until the sound of a motorbike ripped into the quietness making him sit up. Raj – shouting at him when he had walked round Yanna Lake on the evening of Holi. Beautiful Yanna, where he had had his best thoughts, where even during the monsoon the light was radiant, while in Amsterdam it seemed, other than for a few months in summer, to be permanently overcast and cold.

Curiosity made him take another slug, then another, another. Soon he had finished half the bottle. And again his head bent to his knees and he stared at an insect moving along the vein of a leaf.

Ordinary humans are scorpions and lizards.

What a strange line that was, making him wonder if the soul The Philosophy likened to a diamond was a different shape or size or quality in a person who had never encountered Aramani. Might the liquid he had just drunk change his soul into a lizard, an insect, something different and less than the jewel it had once been?

'You're losing your head, Kasper.'

The words spoke into his mind; he no longer cared by whom. Instead, he tried to decipher the writing on the bottle. V.O.D.K.A. Out loud, the word sounded like a country. A part of Russia, a corner of Europe. Beneath the word VODKA, the writing was illegible so he took another swig.

Buy water. Drink water. Lean against the trunk of a tree and breathe.

Once more, he had no idea from where the instruction

came. Still, he returned to the store and looked for the same coloured liquid in row upon row of plastic bottles. Breaking open their packaging, he took one bottle out, then, realising his mistake, went to the counter where single bottles were lined up for almost the same price. Three, he placed on the counter, relieved that there was money enough to buy this new cure for his mind.

This time he lay on the grass, let the cold seep into his spine and looked up at the sky, roofs of nearby buildings, fences, canals. And what he longed for most was to see a lion or a monkey, a being without boundaries which could leap wherever it wished.

When he woke it was dark and he had no idea where he was. The park was empty as if, like a shop, it had its own closing time. Only in summer did its life stretch into the night, people sitting around chatting in groups. He had no idea of the time and didn't care. Only knew he must get back to the flat, her flat, a flat, anywhere that was inside and warm.

His legs were heavy as he pulled himself up. He gave into their pace, the movement calming him although he was frozen to the bone. When he reached the building where his life had been broken and re-shaped, he looked up at the window from which he had so often studied the street below. The light was on. A figure moved backwards and forwards, bending low then stretching up. Who was it? Not Hanneke. He had come to know the exact way in which she moved and it wasn't like this: hefty, practical, methodical or else a figment of his drunken imagination.

He entered the building, wishing there was an

escalator, zipped teeth or not, then plodded upstairs and let himself in.

What greeted him was Christmas in a foreign language, laughter and unpacking.

'What's happening?' His address was directed to the air while Hanneke pointed to the man he had stayed with for one night so many years ago – he who had chaperoned him to his first appointment. How stupid that word 'appointment' sounded now.

'Kasper, good to see you.' And the welcome was warm and open and his mind fell over. Through the confusion, he knew only one thing: he wanted a shower and to brush his teeth, not with fingers and ash but toothpaste and the small green brush he had been using for months – 'I use an electric one.' He remembered these words Hanneke had spoken on his first visit to Amsterdam and how he had wondered if all Westerners used something so sophisticated to perform this small task of cleansing.

When he returned to the main room which one day he had measured out, as he had as a child the road by the number of white lines that marked it, he was greeted by laughter and boxes.

'What's happening?' His head felt as if it was cracking open.

'Hanneke asked me to set this up for her.'

This was a box, in it a TV, cables; beside it, a pile of rectangular plastic boxes the size of books.

'What are those?'

'Films.'

He was baffled. Films weren't neatly boxed shapes the size of books; they hung in reels of tape from clothes pegs in Amba's darkroom.

'You know Henry.'

And with the mention of his name, Kasper lost all control.

'Of course I know Henry. I've stayed with Henry. And I know you know Henry. But all this time you haven't talked about Henry so I haven't talked about Henry. Perhaps it's time we did talk about Henry. He never did write that letter to Aramani about leaving, as far as I remember. But I suppose he must have left?'

'We've all left.'

'I'll go.' And Henry closed the door behind him.

'I haven't left.'

'*What?*'

'I haven't left.

'Of course you have. You left just now. Where have you been, Kasper?'

Where he had been and what he'd done 'just now', he was too ashamed to reveal. Besides, his claim still to be a resident of Aramani catapulted him for a second time back to Yanna. How lovely, how perfectly shaped and distinct the lake was compared to the canals that squared off each part of Amsterdam in an endless brackish maze.

'Your trouble is that you live in your mind. Look at yourself, Kasper! You wear expensive clothes, have sex, or try to, get up late and now you've started drinking! And you say you haven't left! But never mind because look what we have now! Thanks to Henry. A TV.'

His silence was livid. If one person couldn't provide her with what she needed – the love or excitement, the peace – she never did what she claimed to have learnt from The Philosophy which was to find what she needed from inside herself. Instead she demanded help from some stooge. And his upset, surprisingly, wasn't just because she had picked up with her old lover but because she had brought into the quietness a box full of noise.

For Kasper, objects had always carried meaning. The lift, Hanneke's flat, its walls and floors, its paintings and sparse furnishings, her precious bedroom where he had learnt the peculiar first moves of physical love, the fact of his own unexpressed sexual tastes and the mistake he had just made... All these he held in his gaze as if over time they had become a part of his own body.

When he tried explaining this to Hanneke, she snapped at him that he couldn't go round making everything he saw into a part of himself. That's what babies did!

'You know nothing about love,' she shouted. 'You might have posed as a self-styled guru in Aramani but here *you're nothing*! So why don't you go and meditate until you've calmed yourself down.'

'Calmed *myself* down!'

'Yes and you can send some calming thoughts my way because I feel like shit.'

Kasper flinched. In her anger, she was breaking all they had loved about language and silence. Perhaps, he thought wildly, it was the baby who was doing the breaking...

But theirs was a special baby.

A Traveller.

'How do we know that? How do we know it isn't some kind of monster born of our sin?'

To this cruelty he found himself walking out for a second time when what he longed to do was lie down and sleep; for a second time too, he took money from her purse. The equivalent of over two thousand rupees.

39

The words that stayed with him as he left were those which accused him of knowing nothing about love. He had learnt at a very young age how a casual comment could make the mind reel; when spoken by an intimate friend the impact caused a fracture that might never fully mend. He remembered, too, what Amba had told him: that he was afraid of involvement. It was true; he didn't like involvement because involvement meant that what mattered to him was always in danger of being injured.

By now it was late and he longed for a bed. In the early evening he checked into a cheap hotel. But as soon as night fell and the sounds of the tourists had died down, he collided once more with a fast, uncontrollable side of himself, more overwhelming than any external noise. On and on it went, spewing out questions: Why did he know nothing about how the world worked? Why had he bought such a dangerous substance earlier in the day? Why didn't he understand women? What was the difference between his feelings for Hanneke and his feelings for Lars? Why hadn't they dealt with the matter of Henry earlier? Was it possible to keep up a belief that wasn't intrinsic to the place where you lived? Could you walk round with grandiose imagery in your head and still live in the world?

Questions beget weariness. Alone and uninterrupted, the solitude he had always told himself was the solution to all problems now failed to come to his aid so that just after midnight, when in India they would be preparing for their first meditation, he forced himself up and in a crazily sung insult accused his old home of sending him mad.

Then taking his key, he walked out into the night. While he wanted to know where he was, he also wanted to be lost, to run into the road and be struck down. With no idea of his location, he allowed the darkness to guide him. Sounds of laughter, glasses, flirtation... Let him be in the midst of these rather than stuck in his own filthy thoughts, like a person underwater!

After twenty minutes he was indeed lost in a maze of narrow roads, in which groups of people of all ages loitered and laughed. At a small supermarket he bought another two bottles, this time in brown, which the vendor opened for him with a contraption that looked like something you might use to crack nuts. He drank as he walked, and the medicine had a different kind of bitterness to the one he had drunk earlier.

On either side of the road were shop windows, in each a woman, two women... Hanneke had mentioned this place but had said he would hate it. Why? Why should he hate it? It was a fascinating spectacle. The fact of each woman having her own small space, her own design, colour, shape, made him wish he'd brought paper. He suddenly forgot everything and, safer standing than moving, stopped dead and stared. Their power, how they taunted the men on the other side of the glass, as if it were they who were rich and the customers poor! Their bodies looked nothing like those of the street women described by The Philosophy; these were beautiful beings in full possession of themselves, nails long and lurid, breasts perfect and fulsome. He wanted to stare at each individually but when one saw him and scratched at her window like a cat trying to claw him, he felt suddenly afraid.

'Cigarette?'

He spun round.

'Interesting, isn't it? Quite a feast if you like that kind of thing.'

'What are you doing here?'

Seeing Lars outside the café was confusing. If Kasper shouldn't be here, even less so should Lars.

'Yes.'

'Yes what?'

'Yes, it's interesting.'

'Good atmosphere.'

'Is it?'

'What happened? Can I help?'

At these words Kasper was stunned. It was the first time anyone had ever asked him such a question. And in the voice of a man who had housed him for hour upon hour while he sketched and learnt to read, it came in the form of a hug followed by an invitation spoken in a rush by his own voice.

'Lars, come back with me.'

'Why here?'

'I had to get out. Be on my own.'

Lars pointed to himself, a half smile on his face.

'I didn't know I was going to bump into you. I

couldn't sleep.'

Seeing Lars seated on the side of the bed, so relaxed, Kasper moved to the chair in the corner of the room wondering if this wasn't the moment to open his life out before a man who was accepting and free. But just as he was about to start, Lars looked into his eyes.

'I know.'

'Know what?'

'About everything. Who you are.'

Kasper stared.

'Come here.'

Side by side.

No movement.

Heart racing.

'You've been drinking.'

'Yes. For the first time.'

'Why?'

'Do you drink?'

'Of course. I've been drinking since I was twelve.'

Kasper raised his gaze to the window. Twelve! When he was twelve all he had drunk was water and milk, occasionally tea. At twelve he didn't even know that alcohol existed.

Then with no attempt to turn towards him, Lars placed the palm of his hand against Kasper's stomach. The heat calmed him, as if a hand positioned there was exactly what he had needed his entire life. In Aramani, as a child, Elders had touched his head, never his body.

'Breathe more deeply.'

For the instruction being so spoken so gently, Kasper obeyed.

'Deeper still. You're all on the surface.'

'Not in my mind I'm not.'

'Shhh.'

And while his head began spinning and the room was suddenly upside down, his body began to calm down.

'What's happening?'

Now Lars turned towards him, pulled him into his arms as if he was a child and Kasper burst into tears.

'What's happening?' he asked again.

Lars said nothing, simply held him, stroking his back and speaking in Dutch. On and on he moved his hand from the back of Kasper's neck to the base of his spine until finally, at ease against such a strong body, Kasper slept in his arms.

When he woke, he was under the bedcovers alone.

40

At eight the next morning, he checked out of the hotel and returned to the flat.

Walking up the stairs, he was surprised at his relief. His home was here, not in a hotel room in the arms of a virtual stranger although he knew as he thought this that he was lying. Lars was no stranger!

He let himself in quietly, thinking Hanneke might be sleeping. But the flat was empty, kitchen tidy, bed made, the whole place cold and inhospitable.

In his panic he forgot he was hungry. Instead, the feeling of being lost which had begun the previous afternoon made him move fast from one room to another. Then suddenly he lay down, raised one leg in the air, as Amba had taught him, then the other, calling his friend's name out loud. And as if the name alone carried an answer, he knew he must drink something hot. But an hour passed before he moved to the kitchen where he noticed a bowl full of oranges. Again, his mind leapt back to Banhi and punishment, and the dreams he had had as a boy. Furious, he took one, ripped off its skin and ate it fast, juice pouring down his chin like tears.

It was after six of the worst hours he could remember that Hanneke returned. And not on her own.

'Hi, Kasper, good to see you again.'

Henry.

Such casual words! This easy, confident man with whom Hanneke had made love laughed in a way she never did with him. Kasper stared at him, eyes as wide and unblinking as a madman's.

'You okay?'

'I'm always okay.' The words carried neither weight nor meaning.

'It smells in here.' Hanneke's voice was cross.

'Don't worry, Kasper. I'm only here to help get the TV working.'

'I thought you'd already done that.'

'There was a cable missing.'

Neither asked where Kasper had spent the night.

Kasper didn't move, either to look at Hanneke or shake Henry's hand. Instead he contracted his energy into a tiny bomb in the depths of himself and froze as they laughed, crawled across the floor, flung pieces of polystyrene in the air. Were they wanting the flat to snow? Why didn't they speak in English rather than fill the air with Dutch, spoken in the tenor either of lovers or very close siblings?

Had he not found his foray into the outside world so coldly unnerving, he would have gone out for a third time, but he knew that for some reason he had to be present to witness the assembling of this household object; had to remind himself he'd got everything wrong; this wasn't, after all, his home.

Still, he envied Henry. Had he seen him in this mode in Aramani, he would have judged him superficial, utterly

201

ill-equipped to deal with the end of a world, above which Kasper thought he would be held so simply, so dearly. Here, Henry was an image of happy-go-lucky competence while Kasper couldn't even bear a flat strewn with cardboard.

That night he and Hanneke shared the same bed. Tiredness dragged him down, his head pounded and the dark seemed never to form fully but to hover in a rainy charcoal grey over chair, dressing table, paintings of the sea, the sky and one of a sun brighter than the actual sun. It was then that he knew that he wasn't the only one to be unhappy; Hanneke was also worrying. And the silence went on until finally the effort of sustaining it overcame them and they dropped into sleep, Kasper to a dream of some cramped underground place where insects crawled along the lines of a leaf.

Then the dream switched and he was back in Aramani, walking up the hill from Yanna Lake. When he reached Aramani's gates they were padlocked. Through the bars he saw hundreds of people in a pyramid-like formation, three to a row: Anouka, Viraj, and Gayan at the summit, others below, old Banhi, flat on the ground. From his elevated position, Gayan brandished the silver cup from which he had drunk when Kasper had visited him in his cottage. 'It's rose water,' Gayan said, then shook drops of its contents on all those beneath him. In the dream, Kasper couldn't remember what flowers Gayan had told him his water had once contained. Nor did he care about roses. They had so often been quoted in clichéd reassurances: *a rose is a rose, it has no need to change itself* when the fact was they were always being urged to change. What he wanted instead was to tell Gayan how much he missed him, how lost he was, how confused…

'Where are you?'

The sound of the words spoken out loud must have woken Hanneke because the next thing he knew her arms were around him.

'I'm here, Kasper!'

While he felt guilty that it wasn't she he'd been summoning, it showed him a need in Hanneke that he had long hoped to see. And yet not one he felt this evening, for Lars and what they had shared in the hotel had disrupted all desire.

41

It was after the meeting with Henry and his night with Lars that Kasper allowed himself to visit the café more often and watch as his friend wiped glasses, poured coffee, tea, beer, slinging a towel over his shoulder as if life was as simple as drinking from a stream. How he admired the strength in his friend's shoulders and loved the sense that, had he asked, Lars could have lifted him high in the air, as Gayan had, Amba, once even Viraj…! He loved, too, the physical shape of Lars' arms, the rounded muscles of his chest, visible through the white T-shirt he wore daily. The same garment the Aramani brothers wore but never showing their upper arms in public, much less their chests. Instead the shape of their bodies was concealed beneath white cotton tunics that fell to their knees.

Kasper wondered how Lars, who seemed to do nothing but stand all day, had come to be as he was.

'You're interested in how I got my muscles,' Lars joked.

'How did you know I was thinking that?'

'You mentioned it the other night, remember?

'Did I? What else did I say?'

'Nothing, my love.'

My love?

Kasper stared at him, wondering what had actually happened during the night Lars had spent with him in the hotel but didn't dare ask. Instead, he pointed his pencil straight at Lars' left eye.

'No, a little higher. There. That's where my soul is.'

'How do you know about souls?'

'I've had my experiences just as you've had yours. Drugs, classes, working out three times a week.'

'I work things out every day, every minute, every second.' And suddenly tears rose once more into Kasper's eyes at the sense of how little that hard work had served him – his body, so slim and feminine, so slight.

'I could get two fingers round your wrist!' Lars joked. Then seeing Kasper's upset, he put his arms around him and held him close.

'You're beautiful, Kasper.'

'Me?'

'Well, I'm not talking to the towel!' Lars flicked the cloth that hung down Kasper's back. 'You're beautiful. You just need to develop more strength. Come with me. I'll show you.' And he flexed his arm and laughed.

'Come with you?'

'To my place. I can take a visitor. You sit about too much.'

Kasper had no idea how to respond to this invitation but the word spoke itself for him.

'Alright.'

From the little he knew of gyms, they were large, unfriendly places that smelt of rubber and cheese and were filled with great humps of brown leather designed to be leapt over.

As a small child in England, he had never been asked to jump or roll or leapfrog but he had seen older boys at it and been put off.

'In here,' said Lars, unlocking a door two streets away from the café.

'It looks like a house.'

'It's mine!'

At the top of a flight of stairs was a large room to the right and a second to the left, filled with lockers and mirrors. Lars chucked him a pair of jogging bottoms and a T-shirt.

'They smell of you.'

Lars laughed, smelt his bundle of clothes and kissed his own fingers.

'Where do we change?'

Kasper looked down.

'The toilets are over there if you prefer.'

Much later, when thinking of Lars, it was this moment almost as much as any other he had spent with the man that stayed in Kasper's mind; the kindness of someone who knew Kasper took no pride in his body, and the fact that he didn't laugh at him when he emerged in clothes that didn't fit.

'We'll start with the exercise bike. Get on this one. I'll be beside you.'

Again it was the words Kasper hung on to – *I'll be beside you.*

Lars selected the speed. Terrible music blared into the room as Kasper worked his legs up and down.

'I'll make the incline higher.'

What did incline mean, Kasper wondered, while *higher* reminded him of Aramani.

'More?'

'More.'

A second adjustment was made so that his legs could barely move.

'Concentrate.'

'What?'

'Don't think so much. Focus on your legs.'

'It's the music.'

'Take no notice. Just think of your feet.'

After five minutes, Lars led him to another machine, on which he was instructed to sit, hands holding two black loops.

'Weights. Light to begin with.' And Lars placed what looked like two blocks of gold wrapped in black plastic on the machine beside him and told him to stretch out his legs then pull down with his arms. Kasper remembered how, in one of the most bizarre scenes he had witnessed in Aramani, Anouka had been lifted onto a set of scales. She stood on one side; on the other, multiple gold bars were piled up in order to match her weight. The more the bars, the bigger the cheer.

'What's wrong?'

'I'm sorry. I was thinking about something.'

Lars stood down from the weights machine, came round and knelt before Kasper.

'Too hard?'

Kasper nodded.

'Everything too hard? Let's make it easy then.'

And with one of the weights removed, Kasper's arms flew up like wings.

'You won't gain any muscle if it's that easy. Sometimes, things need to be hard.' And Lars sat down and explained to Kasper how the muscles had to tear and rebuild themselves; that this was how weight-lifting worked.

And suddenly the days became filled with colour. Sometimes, Kasper stole more money from Hanneke's purse, drank beer, walked around the streets, lay in the park and twice more, Lars took him to the gym.

With new experiences of his own, Kasper found it easier to accommodate Hanneke's moods, although into the depth of his mind where he had worked so hard to cultivate virtue, criticism lurked heavy. While he was thinking of the feel of Lars' body against his, on and on she went about where it would be right for the baby to live, what sort of upbringing he should enjoy, whether she should give up work, and if so where the money to live on would come from….

When the sound of their combined thoughts became unbearable, he closed his eyes and, selecting one place after another in Aramani, tried to keep his focus that way while Hanneke subdued her anxiety by watching TV.

One early morning, when he was thinking about Lars, she turned to him in bed and asked him if he loved her. His first reaction was to recoil. But it was quicker to lie, so he held her face close to his and told her that he did, of course he did.

Her next words were spoken in a tone of total detachment.

Kasper, the baby might not be yours.

He leapt up from the bed so that he was standing over

her.

'Say that again.'

'The baby might not be yours. I mean, you weren't exactly – '

'Exactly what?'

But he knew what she meant; he had no skill in bed, not in her bed at least.

'As for you saying *might* about a child. I hate the word *might*. If the baby only might be mine then it, *he* might as well be someone else's. In fact, he is someone else's!'

'We don't know that.'

'So why did you mention it?'

'To warn you.'

And into the silence, she began telling him that she and Henry had had sex since he'd been in Amsterdam.

'So why did you ask me to live with you if you still loved him? What was the reason for bringing me here to a city I knew nothing about if you didn't love me? Why did you convince me to leave Aramani?'

She turned onto her side.

'You're different...now you're here.'

'You mean without my position and my white uniform which you were so keen I get rid of?'

'Everything you did was your own choice.'

Here, he was caught. Hadn't he spent years preaching self-reliance and the futility of blaming others?

'Why didn't you tell me about Henry?'

'I assumed you already knew. You read my letter about him. But you were so proud of your solitude and your role as postmaster – which let's not forget you abused – that you didn't own up to the fact that it mattered to you. You should have asked.'

Shocked, he forced her to face him, sought out her eyes, and just when he was about to brave the darkness of hurt, he obliterated her.

'I'm leaving.'

42

Recalling the brutality of those words, which described the way he rid himself of all problems, Kasper stood in his childhood room feeling light-headed. Touch was his instinct. He had used it in the flat in Amsterdam and he used it now: table, mattress, pillow, the brightly coloured quilts that had been bought in the village; tapped one at a time the wide wooden legs of the bed. After that, he moved on to the mustard-coloured armchair, ran his hands along its back, its seat. Then the wardrobe, coat hangers, freshly ironed white clothing on the top shelf, the newspaper that lined it. Finally, the door, the balcony railings from which the mountains were visible.

Returning to the room, he shivered with cold. Good! A feeling he understood and could control.

> *Your greatest enemies are anger and blame. In the time*
> *required to take a single breath, anger and blame will*
> *destroy you forever.*

And it did. It came again. That terrible itching just beneath the surface of his skin.

He swiped at the side of his head as if flicking an insect from his hair, then began the ritual over again. Table, bed,

211

chair, cupboard, coat hangers, clothing...

Finally, a few seconds of peace, easing him of the sensation that beset him so often these days: that everything was both too close and at the same time too far away.

While Kasper had been re-living his time in Amsterdam, thinking about Hanneke, the struggle between his love for her, his commitment to independence and his afternoons with Lars, Anouka had been travelling across India. Leaving his room, he bumped into her in the courtyard. She signalled him to follow her into the room where Amba had given him his first lessons. He had no interest in going, but her power and his vulnerability won him over.

Seated at her feet amid a bunch of white-clad devotees, he listened as she related news of her travels, listing the people of interest she had met: an ambassador's wife, a member of the Indian government, an English aristocrat...

He thought of Lars and how, so often, when sitting with him in the café, Lars had described his travels to places of beauty: long deserted roads, lakes and mountains in Australia, stretches of green and blue in New Zealand, beaches in Bali; how he had ridden the rapids, climbed some of the highest mountains on earth, been deep into caves... The Elders were always talking of travels but, as ever, he noticed Anouka offered no description of the physical features of the places she had visited. It was as if they were the equivalent of bodies to be discarded, while it had occurred to Kasper more than once that it was places which would ultimately endure while their peoples would be wiped out.

After the others left, cheerful and bright, as if each famous name she had mentioned contained hidden within it some potion to free them of sorrow, she beckoned Kasper to follow her, led him beneath an arch of bougainvillea, purple petals falling on her shoulders, and close to the marble square where students sat in the white heat of the afternoon. Then to her room.

Sitting in a deep, plush armchair, her feet on a small stool, she gestured him to sit opposite her.

'What is your trouble?'

The question, put not to his face but to the wall behind him, was one he couldn't risk answering because he could return it only with questions of his own: *Why do you feel the need to boast about people you think important?* And more urgently: *Why did you stop loving me when I wasn't a child anymore?* The first question would have puzzled her for it was her duty to attract the eminent to Aramani; the second, she would either have side-stepped or ignored. So, seated in a room which had once held him so dearly, he played a trick she herself had played on him in the past: took her back to what was practical.

'I'd like to know the cost of my stay here. I want to sort out my budget.'

'Budget?' The word in her voice sounded like an expletive.

'Yes, budget.'

'We do not budget here! Gayan provides.'

'Or a few hundred businessmen from the West.'

'You may put whatever you wish in the donation box before you leave.'

And yet the words *before you leave* unexpectedly upset him. He was as sure as she that he would be leaving soon.

But to be reminded of it so cheerfully was like being a person who, claiming to care nothing for his own birthday, is yet disappointed when no gift is received.

As he emerged into the courtyard, it seemed to him that there was nowhere in Aramani left to go. Banhi was never there, the chair outside her fruit store always empty; Amba, he hadn't seen since their embrace in the garden.

As a child, it was always the courtyard he sought out when lonely or lost. As a very young man it had helped him find his way, either to the centre of himself or the edge that was other people. At twenty, he had used the space as a parade ground, walking silent and mysterious in a way that had attracted admiration.

Today it was empty.

As if committing a sin, he lowered himself into Viraj's chair, stroked its gold lacquered arms feeling, in its warmth and protection, a rush of sadness as if something huge and important had been taken from him. Himself, he supposed. It was always oneself, in the end.

Each person you meet is a mirror.

When this *each* appeared, she broke in as if entering a room without knocking, speaking in that Dutch accent which so unnerved him for he couldn't stand to hear Holland pouring into the Aramani air.

'My name is Alice. I'm a researcher. I've been inviting residents and visitors to talk about their experience of this place. Would you be interested in saying a few words?'

He stood up, took her in as a student, then as a person assessing any good-looking being: dark hair, green eyes, slim body. And he realised she was the girl he had met in the lift and later seen lying by the side of the new hotel pool.

'I'd rather not.'

'That's fine. We only want people who are happy to talk, you know, about the highs and lows of living in such a disciplined way.'

'I'd rather not.'

She raised her hand in a friendly salute then began walking away. But, in his longing for company, he called her back and instead of asking her who she meant by the word *we*, he told her he didn't know what to say.

'Nothing complicated. As I said, just talk a little about what it's like to live here. We want to get a feel of the place. I'm enjoying it, which isn't what I expected. Whenever you're ready. It'll be edited later so it doesn't matter if it's not perfect.'

The word set him off.

'Perfection is the whole problem.'

The camera pointed at him like an unwieldy gun.

'It puts people under too much pressure. Nobody's normal here. There isn't anything normal. There should be. There should be some normality.'

He could say no more.

'Don't worry. That was great. A question though. Apart from perfection, what specifically makes it hard to live here?'

'I didn't say it was hard, it's just –'

The camera went up again.

'Just?'

'It's just that sometimes you reach the end of the road.'

Then down.

'Tell me more.'

'Not now.'

'Later?'

'Maybe.'

The exchange suddenly made him long to see Gayan. To do no more thinking, answer no questions, either from strangers or himself. Instead go to Gayan, sit before him and tell him face to face: *I betrayed you.*

43

Amsterdam 1986.

Lars behind the bar in Café Prins, Kasper at a table.

'You're leaving.'

'How did you know?'

'Hanneke told me.'

'Hanneke?'

'I've known her for years.'

'And you didn't tell me?'

'I did tell you. Anyway, I only answered her questions, nothing else.'

'She seems to know everything.'

'She might think that. But no one knows everything, Kasper. And to be honest, I wouldn't trust her an inch.'

Why had they not had this conversation before? And why did he not have the courage to delve further into this view that was, if given thought, so frightening? Instead, as always, he turned to his art.

'I've brought you these.' And he took from his sketchpad drawings he had kept hidden beneath tissue. 'I'll keep this one; the rest are for you.'

'Where are you going? She didn't tell me that.'

'London.'

'I wish you the best. You're doing the right thing. I'll

217

miss you, Kasper.'

'But -'

Kasper stood up to face him.

Lars raised his hand.

'No, Kasper! Keep it simple. Coming and going. It's only that. Coming, going. That's how I live.'

'But you called me *my love?*'

'You are a love.'

'That's all?'

'It's enough.'

'You need so little?'

'I have plenty.'

To his surprise, while hurt by Lars' neutrality, it was also a help, making for a smoother passage out of the prison Amsterdam had become. But the words that haunted him were those not about love but simplicity. Hadn't The Philosophy said the same?

Keep your thoughts simple and life will be the same.

When Kasper phoned his father, he didn't expect him to answer since he had never replied to his letter. But there he was, quiet-voiced, welcoming, telling him to come when he pleased, he would meet him at the airport. At this warmth Kasper was taken by surprise, while he also wondered if Hanneke hadn't got there ahead of him as she had with Lars; stolen the piece of paper from his wallet and made the initial phone call herself; perhaps even intercepted letters his father might have written to him. For like someone easing a discomfort away, she aided his departure, telling him to take the white kimono he had worn almost daily since their first intimacy, even accompanying him on the tram to the station.

The train to Schiphol was full. Then the flight was delayed. At the prospect of a four-hour wait, Kasper knew he must do things in stages, as he used to in Aramani. First, walk up and down one hundred times, find the nearest screen to sit by, watch as the numbers notched up telling of the changing time of departure, draw a picture then repeat…

Too fast he muddled the order of events, grabbed coffee and a magazine full of photos before drawing a picture of a sleeping child, another of an empty chair, only turning to his thoughts when there was nothing else left.

For the last half hour, he sat in the bright, dead light of the departure lounge. Usually averse to public spaces, that day he wanted to see the planes, so he positioned himself by the window and watched as they took off and landed. This helped him settle, as if these machines with their wings so vast and slow somehow echoed the up and down movements of his own mind.

Once in the air, he thought again what a miracle it was that his father had been there when he called. But he was distressed by the fact that he couldn't picture his face. Still, from the moment of their farewell when he was just seven, he had never forgotten the voice, with its constant mispronunciation of the letter 'w', for which his mother had teased him. One evening, his father had lashed out at her and Kasper remembered feeling outraged that it was he who was sent to his room, when it was his mother who was in the wrong.

Arriving at Heathrow and spotting his father holding up a piece of card labelled with his name – *Kasper Chaudhury* – a shiver of laughter rooted in exhaustion raised Kasper's mood to an airy derision. In seconds, derision turned to irritation. For here was his own nervous self repeated before him, in a being who jumped when he was touched, whipped the card away when Kasper said hello, smiled without his eyes and had a tooth missing.

No more confident himself, Kasper fell back on good manners.

'Thank you for coming to meet me. I wouldn't have recognised you.'

'That's why I brought this.' His father waved the piece of card up and down. Kasper was annoyed that he didn't feel pleased to be in the presence of his own flesh and blood. In fact, as soon as he was in the passenger seat of his father's car, he felt only that his life was about to contract for a third time: Aramani, lift, Amsterdam and now… a cell.

It was close to midnight when they arrived in a place that seemed like a sprawling row of dull-looking buildings, and a semi-detached house which, once out of the car, Kasper saw was a shop window.

'It's a post office.'

The irony didn't pass Kasper by and his first thought, as it tended always to be, was that he was being punished.

After edging their way past a couple of bins, they entered by a side door which led straight into the shop, another to stairs and a sitting room.

'It's small, but you're welcome to stay. Leave your shoes there.'

'They're your shoes.'

'Not any more. Your mother took them to India just after I'd bought them so I forgot about them years ago! Leave them there. And Kasper, since you don't remember me well, which isn't your fault, don't feel you have to call me Pop as you did when you were little. You can use my name. Surya.'

Hearing these words of appeasement, Kasper felt only confusion about this man who was his father and yet seemed so small and so bumbling.

In fact, this was a misreading. Surya Chaudhury was neither of these. He too had bad thoughts, and sometimes was as sharp as Kasper in his retorts. When Kasper asked him if he needed help making tea, he was met with a bark.

'Do you think I can't make such a long-awaited visitor tea?'

That night, Kasper yearned to be back in Hanneke's flat, or alone in a room somewhere, anywhere… To be away from this minuscule house that was dingy and thin, with its polycotton sheets and Artex ceilings. He sensed, too, that here he would find it hard to think clearly. There would be work to do, and once begun, it would be tricky to get away.

He got everything wrong during those first few days, staying almost exclusively in the box room that Surya had turned into his bedroom. He offered a combination of excuses – shock, travel, the time needed to adjust. But he soon realised that, after a childhood of freedom, Surya expected a fair exchange of labour for accommodation.

Then there was the dog – an animal Kasper had begged for as a child. But in his teenage years, he had gone by The

Philosophy which taught that animals were dirty. Unable to re-connect with his childhood self which had so loved the keening of the dogs in the wild, the village donkey and the idea of tigers, he found this lolloping domestic animal a nuisance. It was too big, too restless, kept jumping up, scratching at his legs, lying in doorways; it also needed constant walking. After three days, Kasper kicked it and then the guilt flooded back. So he bent down and stroked it. When it squirmed away, he gave up, for sustaining any kind of effort seemed now entirely beyond him.

On the fourth morning, he ventured out for a walk, hoping that the air and the space might help. Again he jumped too fast to judgements and his verdict on the place was that it was ugly. Delhi was bad, but at least it was warm, busy, colourful: children running everywhere, street salesmen cleaning and repairing people's shoes, tossing chapattis, selling hand-made trinkets…

In contrast, this place, a suburb of London, was a damp mess of streets, full of empty cafés and betting shops, bingo halls, clinics selling Chinese medicines that looked like black mushrooms. There was only one spot he liked: a vegetable stall where the apples and oranges were stacked in pyramids of bright colour. But the girl behind the counter, with her very short hair and studded upper lip, was no more like Banhi than his father was like a resident of Aramani.

Although Surya seemed uninterested, Kasper kept hoping that if he spilled his heart, this dogged little man with his biros and form-filling would wake up and tell him why he had lacked the guts to come after his wife and son; explain, too, what had happened to him during the time they'd been apart. But the constant flow of his talk was fixed only on the present: form-filling, food, lists, tasks. It was a special moment, then, when he offered his most delicate revelation.

'I'm not well, Kasper. That's why I need your help. I have Parkinson's disease. It's in its early stages but I often feel weary.' And he held out his hands which shook even as he tried to steady them. 'So you could help me.'

The simplicity of the statement floored Kasper, but duty spoke his answer. Of course he would help until he decided what to do next with his life. Surya responded that it would take more than a few months to get Kasper a licence to work in the post office, and for now would he please support his assistant in the shop: a middle-aged woman – Magda.

So... Honesty and endurance were no longer words simply to be painted or described; they were qualities he was required to live out in action. As for the notion of paying for his keep, Kasper had no understanding of the matter, and no money either.

It was also with terrible disappointment that he saw Surya had no interest in his story. He asked him enough to confirm that he'd left Aramani to live with a woman in Holland, but no more. Perhaps inscrutability was a family trait. Still, Kasper felt resentful. This was his father; he should be interested. There again, according to The Philosophy, which he realised he hadn't even begun

223

to shake off, the best thing a person could do was keep himself to himself. Wasn't this how he treated people? Yet, on the receiving end of such indifference, he was bereft.

44

Afternoon of his thirtieth day back in Aramani.

With no destination in mind, Kasper ambled once more across the courtyard, ending up at the small souvenir shop just inside the front gates which sold touched-up photographs of Gayan, notebooks, pens and key rings bearing instructive slogans. He used to look down on visitors when they became greedy over such trinkets, although he had also understood because in his own way he too had been a collector of small things.

As he walked on past the shop, he saw the woman who had interrogated him the day before.

'Hi. No camera this time.' She held out her palms. He was going to ignore her but his mind collapsed, words spilling from his lips.

'Which city are you from?'

'Amsterdam.'

At the mention of Amsterdam, his mind reared up.

Had she been to the studio there? Yes, on and off over the last year; she had an interest in The Philosophy but not in total self-sacrifice, which is what The Philosophy seemed to demand. Anyway, if there were such a being as God, surely he wouldn't deny people the right to enjoy life, or make loving him so complicated, or state that only a certain number of people could make it to heaven.

'What's the point in being a half-hearted student? You don't gain anything that way. You should either study properly or not at all.'

'I don't see why. What about people who aren't blessed with brains? Isn't your god interested in them too?'

Her comments carried no aggression, only an openness which in the past he would have seen as weakness.

Perhaps there was a choice in life after all? Perhaps it wasn't of such importance whether one studied or not; perhaps nobody stood on the other side of death with a stick to beat you if you had missed a few early morning meditations or taken too few baths in a day.

'As I say, it's my experience that you can only gain from The Philosophy if you go into it in depth. If you don't study, you're like someone swimming in the shallows.'

'I can't swim.'

'Nor can I,' he said, irritated at this return to the literal.

Then suddenly, as if for her connection to Amsterdam he must keep her close, he asked if she'd like tea.

'No thanks. I was thinking of going into the village for a cold drink, if you'd like to come?'

'Do you know Hanneke?'

'I've met her at the studio.'

'She still goes to the studio?'

'Now and then. When she can get someone to look after the children. Her husband's busy.'

'Husband? *Children*?'

'Yes to both.'

'I'll come to the village.'

Instinctively, Kasper decided to take her the back route rather than walk the road that circled Yanna, the lake with which he associated some of his most treasured times of study.

First, they returned to the courtyard where Viraj was sitting with his newspaper.

'What is it?' she asked.

'I don't like being watched.'

'Do you think people are watching? Aren't most people here thinking about themselves?'

His voice was sharp for Alice's observation hit a nerve. Perhaps she was right. Perhaps he was of no importance to anyone but himself?

By this time, they had left Aramani and were walking through the villagers' camp. He stared at her back as she walked, hating her for robbing him of what little of the outside world he had ever had.

When they reached the market, his mood became reckless. Two bottles of lemonade between them, heads bent forward to drink.

'Is Hanneke married to Henry?'

'Henry?'

'No?'

'He's called Dirk.'

'And she's Hanneke?'

'Yes.'

Kasper's breathing became shallow. Fizz poured from his mouth and onto the table. She stretched out her hand, held his wrist tight. He hit at his chest and coughed.

'Thank you. What colour hair does the older child have?'

'Why? Is he yours?'

'Nobody's mine. If you understood The Philosophy you'd understand that you don't even belong to yourself.'

'If a child is your child he's your child! You can't disown a child. That seems to be the whole problem with this place. It either exploits children or neglects them. And what about your life? How old did you say you were when you were dumped here?'

'Exploit? Nobody's exploited in Aramani! And I wasn't dumped here. I came with my mother when I was seven and I was happy. What colour is his hair?'

'Red.'

'So he's Henry's child.'

'His name's Casper. With a C.'

The look on Kasper's face had the astonishment of someone trying to understand a new word.

'Do you want me to give her a message when I get back?'

Two kites wheeled above them. Kasper watched as they formed figure eights in the sky.

'Do you believe everything they teach you here?'

The question rescued him from the beginning of a horrible pain.

'Yes.'

'Even the idea that God inhabits Gayan? You really believe that?'

'It doesn't matter whether it's God or Gayan. What matters are the words spoken. The rest is detail... People always want to destroy us when they don't understand.'

'Us? I thought you'd left.'

'I'm here, aren't I?'

'What about the fact that the group splits up families?'

'Who says it splits up families?'

'Well, it's not just a question of celibacy, is it? It's about solitude, non-attachment; it says going to films is wrong, reading is wrong, meeting ordinary people is wrong, that ordinary people, as you call them, are in fact wrong about everything. That's a lot of wrongs, don't you think? And what about people who leave? How do they cope? Do they get permission to go or do they just run away?'

Now he was furious.

'Look, I'll tell you one thing. Forget what you don't understand and stop asking so many questions. Questions destroy your peace.'

'That's a dangerous way to live, don't you think, not asking questions?'

'It's the only way to live.'

He was relieved, walking back through the village when she became distracted by the shops.

'I love all this stuff. They sell this kind of fabric for a fortune in the West. I'd like to get a whole new set of clothes here but I've already got too much stuff.'

'I imagine you have.' He heard the malice in his voice and grieved for his soul.

45

Kasper woke the next morning knowing something awful had happened but couldn't recall what. Then he remembered the girl. Alice. How he'd sat with her in the village and she had told him things that made him see that, if he had cut Hanneke off in words, his heart still held on to the promise of the free life she enjoyed. And yet with that promise broken, another kind of freedom was restored. Whatever Anouka had said about him leaving, he had a right to take Aramani back. To talk to Amba, ransack the kitchens, see Banhi again, spy on the horrible Kala, enjoy the wide expanse of the place, even love it.

With something to pit himself against, a day which might have been difficult suddenly became easier.

Having no lift to operate, he made a pilgrimage in the way he had told the businessmen to in his lecture; returned to each meditation room, the khejri trees, the courtyard, the banyan tree at the end of the road that led to Yanna Lake. He even went to the village and back. And in one place after another, the sensation he registered most clearly came through his hands: the walls of each meditation room, the texture of the cloth that covered the surface of things, the bark of every tree, the cool of the seating area that surrounded the courtyard, the hard of the stone and the soft of the cotton cloth that made up the padded floor of the large hall he had sat in a day earlier… Only the gaudy cartoons that illustrated The Philosophy did he ignore, for he hated them as much as he had as a child.

In the late evening, when the residents were in their rooms and darkness had fallen, he set off in the direction of Amba's shed.

From a distance he was able to make out the water jars on the wall, their overlays removed for the night, make-shift lids in their place. Gadgets and tools lay strewn about outside, and a small lantern was fixed to a newly-designed lintel above his door.

Kasper whispered Amba's name, relieved finally to be saying it out loud rather than just thinking it, then tapped on the closed door. In pursuit of his childhood, he dodged to one side and pressed his nose against the window. The face inside moved away. He went back to the door and shoved it with his foot.

'What do you want?'

'You! I want to see you, Amba!'

'Well, here I am.'

Inside, Kasper saw that the whole place had changed. It was indeed a little house of its own. There was a proper bed with a pink and blue quilt like the ones on sale in the village, a table and lamp on a strong silver base…

'I was asleep.'

'Amba. Look at this! You've got a real house. How did that happen?'

Dressed in his nightshirt, Amba finally let him in. Kasper took the wooden chair by the window from which shawls and Kurtas drooped as if carelessly discarded. The two men stared at each other.

'I was asleep.'

'Yes, you said. But what about here? How did you get all this?'

'Aramani isn't as it was.'

'I can see that. You're living in luxury. I went up to that place with the swimming pool the other day Who owns that? And what happened to your massage shed?'

As he spoke, Kasper felt himself trying to fall back into childhood yet knowing that the door to the past was now closed.

'Gayan owns the hotel. He lets it out to visitors.'

'Aren't you pleased? All this!'

'Yes, I like *all this*,' said Amba, gesturing to the room.

'So Aramani's modernising itself. That's a good thing.'

'Maybe.'

'Maybe not?'

For a little they were quiet and Kasper sensed that he would never be able to reach his old friend again. In glimpses perhaps, the occasional caress but not in any sustained way. At which thought, Amba picked up a glass of water.

'Red,' he said. 'I was going to drink it but it's you who needs it not me.'

Kasper took it, his heart banging.

'If you stay it will be hard. I mean it, Kasper! You should leave!'

This tendency to predict was one of the things Kasper had always disliked about Aramani. It was, he decided, a way of frightening people, to tell them the future would always hold sorrow.

'How's Kala treating you these days?'

Amba smiled, sniffed, then slowly shook out his handkerchief and faked a sneeze.

The joy this gesture provoked exceeded all words.

But in the space of a second it was destroyed as Kasper saw tears gathering in Amba's eyes.

'Leave. Go, Kasper!'.

'But I'm hungry!'

'You've lost your passport.'

'It's in my rucksack.'

'Not that passport! I mean you can't just have what you want any more.'

'I knew what you meant.'

'The kitchens will be locked. I've got a bag of sweet rotis.'

'The milk room, Amba. What's happened to the milk room? Anil. Puki. Where are they?'

'People come and go these days.'

'No, Amba! They'd been here for years. People who've lived here for years don't just disappear.'

Amba's face was blank. As if he was dead.

'I was a child, Amba. But the twins were adults; they were happy.'

'I don't know the story. All I know is that they don't make tea with leaves anymore.'

'Teabags,' said Kasper through a mouthful.

'Except on Wednesdays.'

Amba picked up an old camera from the table by his bed and peered through its lens.

'Broken.'

'What do you do these days? Are you still developing photos?'

Amba put the camera down.

'Every day.'

'The Elders?'

'Gayan mainly.'

'Aren't there enough pictures of Gayan?'

'He's developed other interests. Wants other photos.'

'Of?'

'You'll have to ask him. I don't know. I just do what I'm asked to do.'

Hearing his friend's voice so unyielding, once more Kasper felt a terrible sadness. He wanted him as he had been on the scooter, in the teaching room, at the temple... And most of all, when on his return he had allowed himself to be free of Aramani's rules and kissed him.

In this confusion of needs, he asked for more food. This time, Amba joined him, taking his customary chomp from the thick pastry biscuit.

'I'm glad I've seen you properly, Amba. And Banhi. Tell me about Banhi.'

'Banhi.'

'Amba, take me to her. I've tried finding her but she's never in her fruit store. I keep going there and it's empty. And now the lift's broken -'

Amba laughed. As if Kasper had understood nothing.

'She has a room of her own too. And someone to look after her.'

'They were laughing at her in the dining room on my first morning back.'

'They don't mean anything by that.'

'I want to see her.'

'I'll take you,' said Amba, fiddling once more with the camera. 'I'll meet you in the courtyard at midday tomorrow. Then you'll see why you should leave!'

46

At midday, Kasper walked up the road to the gates and into the courtyard. Amba sat hunched on the bottom step that led up to the room where he had given Kasper his first lessons.

He spoke fast. 'We'll go to her now.'

Kasper longed to hold him, feel his warmth. But he was living in a play that had a script and stage directions. And the directions instructed distance. Still, no one could stop the improvisation of thought. And the thought, as they walked side by side in the direction of Gayan's cottage, was this:

> *If for no one but Amba and Banhi, I'd be happy to stay in Aramani.*

Since his return he had only been to the cottage once and that once, Gayan had told him he was too busy to talk.

'I'm not in the mood to see Gayan, Amba.'

'I know.'

'Why are we here then?'

'Because this is where she lives.'

'This' was a newly-built bungalow set a few yards back from where Gayan stayed.

'A granny flat,' said Kasper, a term returning to him from something Magda had mentioned one day in the post office in London.

'Precisely,' said Amba.

'No!'

'It wasn't necessary to tell you before.'

'How many concealed facts are there in Aramani?'

'Facts are facts.'

'But why didn't you tell me? When you told me about Kala and Raj, why didn't you tell me everything?'

'Sit down.'

Amba dropped down onto the grass that stretched from the back of Gayan's cottage to Banhi's small bungalow, Kasper beside him.

'When you were a child, you liked to think things and people came from nowhere; that people were just born into Aramani. Why take that from you?'

'Because I'm not a child anymore and because it's a lie!'

'Well, I've told you now. Or you've told yourself. Banhi is Gayan's mother. Fullstop. Now let's go in and see her. She's still Banhi. It's her illness that's the enemy not The Philosophy and not Gayan.'

'Was that why she never came to classes? Because she didn't believe in The Philosophy?'

'I know nothing about that. Everyone in Aramani is different.'

'And what about you? Why did Gayan give you all that smart furniture? The lamp, the bed, and-'

Amba laughed at him as if Kasper had just cracked a joke. Then he pulled him up so that, whatever the answer, Kasper wanted desperately to take him in his arms and hang on to him forever.

'Amba, I wish I'd never grown up!'

'You haven't.'

The woman who came to the door was sallow and unsmiling; she was also familiar.

'You were the person who helped me when I had a back ache.'

She smiled in assent; Kasper looked at Amba then at her and back at Amba. 'She's your sister. Your blood sister? And that's why you've got a nice place to live! Because now everyone's getting old your sister is *useful!* So why does The Philosophy call the body *an old shoe* if it costs so much money to look after it?'

'Be quiet, Kasper. Let's go inside.'

They were shown into a small room with two armchairs, a silver embossed table, and a large photo of Gayan on the wall.

'I made that print.'

'Where's Banhi?'

'Probably asleep,' said the sallow-looking woman.

Amba opened the door. And there she was, sitting up in bed, eyes open but unseeing. Kasper fell on her like a child.

'It's me. Kasper. I saw you in the dining room on my first day back. How are you? Where have you been?'

These were the questions he realised he had longed for someone to ask him: *How are you? Where have you been?*

She said nothing, didn't move, even to his embrace. Amba went up to her, bent down and bellowed. Her face crumpled, top lip touching her nose in a smile.

'How does she eat?' Kasper asked.

'She never wanted new teeth. Everything she eats is mashed up.'

Kasper bent down a second time to hold her and was surprised when she let out a howl of laughter. He longed to stop her, to calm her into silence and feel the texture of her sari as he had as a child. But she was solid now, her nose even bigger than it had been, ears huge and floppy, scalp almost bald.

She said his name and pointed towards a framed photo on the other side of the room.

'I gave it to her,' said Amba.

It was the picture his friend had taken of him in a position of study, pretending to be a guru.

'I kept the other one myself.'

This revelation provoked a surge of joy.

Whatever the warnings issued by Amba:

They're the only family I have.

47

London 1986.

The trouble with living above the post office was the lack either of family or solitude. Rising early was hard, thoughts impossible to compose. And when Surya came down to make tea he turned morning too fast into day with all its fidgeting and papers and its wide white sky which seemed never to brighten.

Again and again, Kasper longed for the outdoor space and crispness of Aramani, the fresh air, the high room... But all that was gone, as if the mode of transport to reach it was broken. He seemed instead to be living in what felt like a waiting room with no appointment to go to.

Other than work.

A few doors from the post office stood a pair of garages. Kasper hadn't noticed them so was curious when one Saturday afternoon, Surya opened the second garage to reveal what he said was his most prized possession: an old sports car.

'We'll go for a ride,' he said.

Climbing in, Kasper noticed a new intensity in Surya's face as if he was enjoying a long-awaited treat. When their destination turned out to be a service station a few miles off the motorway, Kasper was baffled.

'What do you think of this steering wheel?'

'Seems fine?'

'More than fine. And this. Look at this.'

'This' was the mechanism that rolled back the roof.

'If you ever buy a car, Kasper, always buy second-hand. Cars lose their value as soon as they leave the forecourt. And it's important to get an independent mechanic to check before you buy. Also make sure you look at the history in case there's any credit outstanding on it. Then you need to find out whether it has an accident-free – '

Kasper was so bored that his mind interrupted with its own version of how a car should be maintained:

> *Keep checking that the driver has control; that the*
> *car doesn't take over; that the soul is strong, that it's*
> *thinking the right things; that it has enough fuel to*
> *move you through hurts that arise from the past…*

On and on they went, Kasper in silence, his father out loud, until suddenly both lost their way, and into the small space of a car which seemed to Surya as precious as the lift had once been to Kasper, came a rush of entirely different words. How pleased Surya was to have him back, how he felt he had lost him when he'd gone with his mother to India.

'So why didn't you send for me when you sent for Mama? I was still a child then. I went all the way to Delhi with her. It was a long journey. Why did I only go that far?'

'I wanted to speak to your mother alone. I thought it was time we got a divorce. I'd met someone else. I didn't

241

want to deceive your mother even though she'd left me.'

'What happened to her, your *someone else*?'

'I thought your mother looked very thin when she returned from India. I was worried about her.'

'And?'

'I wasn't wrong. She was ill. First it was just a cold. Then endless sneezing. On and on as if she was trying to get something out of her system.'

'*Sneezing?*'

'Yes. But that was nothing compared with –'

'Nothing? Sneezing is never nothing!'

'Then a fever, pain in her gut, hospital…'

'No!'

'Yes, Kasper! She worked too hard in that place. To them illness is just a nuisance. They seem to take no proper care of their bodies.'

'But she said it was you who was ill?'

'That was partly true. As I told you, I have Parkinson's Disease, but she was more seriously ill.'

Kasper sat in glum silence.

'I didn't know anything until they told me. Then we had a ceremony.'

'A ceremony? That's something I suppose. Anyway you were only a child. It wasn't your responsibility. But she went downhill fast. Breast cancer. It spread.'

'But you said it was sneezing!'

'I said that's how it began.'

'And you had to look after her when you weren't well either?'

'I sold our old house. Took on the post office. The sale looked after the cost of her care. Who else did she have? Nobody in that Aramani of yours!'

'And your someone else?'

'It ended.'

'When Mama returned.'

In the months that followed, the life of this man which had felt so small, gave birth to a new awareness in Kasper. Here was a person who lived in relative poverty, in an England where it always seemed to rain, and whose only real love was his sports car. Day after day he was up early, dealing with other people's letters, and what little money he had made from the sale of their family home, he had used to care for a wife who had abandoned him.

One night, Kasper asked him what he found in life to treasure.

'Nothing,' he said. 'I work because I'm alive and I'm alive because I work. I lost my wife, my savings and you. I heard you were in Amsterdam and was sad you didn't write. Yasmin said she had given you my address.'

'Didn't write? I did write!'

'Well, never mind. I found out your address from a contact of my brother's who lives in Amsterdam and Bombay. He said you were living happily with that woman of yours who had left The Philosophy.'

'But I did write to you! I knew I must write and tell you where I was.'

Kasper was livid now with *that woman*. Her trickery, her cruelty!

'And yet you still allowed me to stay with you when I didn't reply?'

'Of course.'

What a man! He had opened his arms to his son

while, perhaps for the purpose of revenge, Hanneke had destroyed any chance for the two men to converse.

> *Whatever you taught us about generosity, Aramani,*
> *you never taught us that kind of sacrifice. You said:*
> *Think of yourself first. What kind of achievement is*
> *that?*

And what was Hanneke thinking, wanting him to live with her and then relieved when he left? What had her motive been?

He remembered Lars' words, which at the time he had resented: *I wouldn't trust her an inch, Kasper. She's an opportunist.* And how, once more, he'd had to ask Lars what the word opportunist had meant.

What anything meant...

48

Kasper lowered his head to the desk and heard his own voice: 'Cry, go on, cry!' But without anyone to witness the performance, no tears came.

I'm as dead as The Philosophy instructed me to be.

He could get up and walk about in an agitated fashion, kick his bed and throw the quilts to the floor. But he couldn't cry. So instead he began laughing. That he had written to Surya and Surya to him and Hanneke had kept the letters for herself, just as he had kept her letters, and those of so many others when they were trying so hard to live by Aramani's rules while still abiding by the rules of the outside world. That Aramani had made him so selfish, that Hanneke's child wasn't his but had been given his name which wasn't his name…

And now everyone around him had lied: Gayan, Kala, Amba, Hanneke. So that The Philosophy was no longer The Philosophy but a set of ideas kept alive by the blood and money of an Indian family. Gayan married to Kala, parents of Raj; Gayan's mother, Banhi; her carer, Amba's sister and Amba the beneficiary of his sister's skills… When everything was meant to be voluntary, just as he'd told Mina and Balvan. And who were they, anyway? Were they relations too? Whatever the case, it seemed to him now that after all his dedication, none of them were living The Philosophy as he had been taught it; instead, they relied on a network of support not from God but each other.

And he had no one.

Yet he, too, was lying.

About something.

But what?

Having wanted to feel, now he wanted to feel nothing. What was the point of emotion? It was only fleeting, after all, while truth was something fixed that held you steady. Experience was not to be trusted either for that was just what a person gathered as they went along when the whole point of life, as he had been taught it, was to be clean. Still, on the page, experience looked like one of the finest words in the language. It involved risk and courage and growing up, which was just what The Philosophy didn't allow because it froze you in time with its maxims and rules.

It was after midnight when Kasper left his room, in search of Aramani as it had been: the light soft, each of its residents slipping alone and distinct into the silence of sleep.

He thought of the swing in the garden close to Banhi's fruit store. It had a double seat; was a place to relax when a break was needed from classes and meetings and the merciless onslaught of the mind.

So it was to the swing that he went for refuge.

As he lowered himself onto its blue upholstered seat, it creaked in a kindly sort of way. His breathing slowed. Footsteps sounded in the courtyard, wild dogs keened in the distance; the breeze rose and fell.

In those moments of ease, Aramani's intensely physical quality was all that he wanted. The fragrance of jasmine, freshly watered grass, something else which he had once known so well and had enjoyed for the whole of his childhood but could identify no more clearly than it being the essence of Aramani herself. She too seemed alive, had gathered her own layers: new buildings, teaching and accommodation blocks, access roads for the vans that brought supplies from Ahmedabad. But the swing had been there from the beginning. The swing was the very soul of Aramani. On the swing he could no more capture the feeling of England than he could of a country he had never visited.

49

London 1988.

A dreary routine set in: helping Surya at collection times, carrying the postal sacks from behind the counter and passing them over to the driver, working in the shop, selling washing up liquid, cards, milk – that milk, which seemed always so mean compared to the vats he'd become used to in Aramani; returning the dry cleaning, the dirty-iron smell of clothing which again he couldn't help comparing with the folded whites he had fetched from the dhobi in the village.

Everything, including himself, he placed against the very ideals he had rejected. When he talked to Magda, like the painting of the old woman's head in Amsterdam, he tried turning her into Bahni. But she wasn't Banhi and she cared nothing for Kasper. Working in a post office wasn't a vocation, it was a job. And at five each afternoon, she went home to another more important life he knew nothing about. Still, when she left, he always felt his angular, unhappy self more acutely. So he tuned instead to Surya's rhythms. Surya also pressed on, shaky hands stamping this, that, the other, shuffling papers, slipping coins into the shallow bowl beneath the counter, fingers meeting the hurried fingers of those in a rush to catch the last post.

And if for some reason Kasper couldn't find the man's real presence, even though he was always nearby, he took comfort in the noises of the shop: the bell above the door, the sound of umbrellas opening and closing, the small talk as people took shelter from the rain and the gales.

In the evenings, when he and Surya were alone, objections were his only company. Surya liked watching TV. Not just certain programmes but anything, everything… Through all sitting, all mealtimes the sound of conversing voices and music filled the space.

'Don't you ever prefer silence?' Kasper asked him one evening.

'Never!'

The ferocity took Kasper by surprise. He wondered whether his father hated silence because he associated it with the very thing that had stolen his wife and child, just as an equivalent rejection had happened in himself with Hanneke. He was ashamed now as he remembered an early conversation they had had about trying to plan a silent birth for *their special child.* What exactly had they thought they were doing when biology dictated the opposite of silence; indeed, the need for both mother and infant to scream?

Sitting in Surya's living room, Kasper tried to picture all this. But it was as if Hanneke's child didn't exist. And that was confusing for if the baby was dead, he should know; if born, he should see it. Yet if he saw it, he knew, should the baby be his, that he'd be weighed down by the responsibility its existence would ask of him.

Thus, Kasper's life continued to contract. Connection with all that he understood to be spiritual seemed slowly to ebb away so that he could no longer locate the method by which to stretch upwards. But if he was dead to Aramani, that dead self knew that something he was doing was right, that he was being shown what people in the outside world had to endure.

Apart from the cinema, where he occasionally succumbed to the escapism of science fiction movies, he made a few casual friends – customers from the shop or members of their families.

Sometimes he wandered the streets, went to the pub, took the dog for walks in the local park. He also opened a bank account although he had little more than the odd twenty-pound note Surya gave him.

In this grey place, Kasper felt himself slipping and slipping, habits growing about him like weeds, whereas in Aramani, the ground had been so clean: no alcohol, no greed, sex, trivia, no possessions…

One evening, as if to keep Aramani close by means of the very substance it claimed to forbid, with two stiff drinks in his system, he told his London acquaintances about his old home.

'So you didn't go to school?'

'Not your kind of school.'

'What did you learn then?'

'How to think.'

The two men opposite him looked at each other; Kasper took no notice; he needed to talk. So out poured an account of Aramani's rules, a description of the khejri trees, the lush green of the mountain, the special light of the very early morning. Listening, they began to show a little more interest but only in passing, as if they were a couple of spectators at a weird film or standing before a strange painting. It was then, with a clarity which pierced through the soft-headed feeling brought on by drink, that Kasper saw how utterly diminishing casual conversation could be; the way it could break in seconds all that a person might treasure.

It was shortly after such an evening that Surya received a letter telling him that the government intended to close his post office down. The old man's reaction alarmed Kasper for it being honesty at its most raw. Once he had become a serious student, he would have changed his clothes at the faintest sign of a stain. And yet like everyone else, he had bragged that he would be alive to witness, unscathed, the blood and anguish of Armageddon. Now, when the news about the post office caused Surya to lose his composure, Kasper was terrified by this image of vulnerability.

He tried to be of help, went down to the shop, explained to customers, now familiar to him, what had happened and how upset his father was. One said Surya was a truly good man, how sorry she felt, another how criminal it was, how typical of the government, how wrong...

When Kasper reported their reactions, Surya simply thanked him then suddenly rose from his quilt, looked Kasper in the eye and said, 'You should go back to Amsterdam. There's nothing of value to keep you here.'

50

Dawn brought wakefulness and thoughts full of Surya. How in the years when he was climbing to stardom, Surya must have been facing the hell of loss, and he, Kasper, had been too busy either to know of his suffering or to care.

He wondered why, when he had met Surya again as an adult, he hadn't asked his father all the questions that seemed so obvious to him now: what kind of *someone else* he had he met and loved after his mother had left? And had she lied about the reason for her return to London? What did she look like when she was dying? Had Surya sat with her in the hospital?

And now it was too late. He could ask him no questions.

At this confusing realisation that it is often in the realm of the ordinary that the real heroes are to be found, he became aware that his mind was moving too fast. On the swing the night before, he had been calm. Now, he was doing the very thing for which he had criticised visitors to Aramani – going over and over what had happened when:

> *The past has passed.*

The thought that still most consumed him, and even

more so after all that he had learnt the day before, was the question of what he should do with his life now. Go back to London? Stay in Aramani? Considering his struggle with the outside world, here was surely where he finally belonged? Or was it a place for infants, capable only of blind obedience to a handful of Elders who were, it turned out, a close-knit clan of their own?

At five-thirty, Kasper forced himself up for the first time since his return, deciding at last he must attend the early morning class he had avoided for the length of his stay. He went into the bathroom for a crouched bucket bath, dressed with care, some unbrokenly faithful part of him hoping to hear in Gayan's words, a phrase, an image, an idea to which he could attach himself and be held by.

Into the silence, the Indian love songs played. They were hauntingly beautiful and the bright sea of white-clad figures rested him, as did the incense which wasn't dusty or dank but smelt of fresh flowers. Even if some were sleepy and others present merely out of duty, the atmosphere was clear and high. After all he had experienced – the homely sounds of Surya's flat, the spacious galleries in Amsterdam, its parks and cafés – he knew that nowhere was as beautiful as this. And the sign of this fact was that his thoughts relaxed into silence.

The hushed expectation, notebooks poised… How deeply he had missed this sense that each day might bring an entirely new way of seeing life.

When Gayan began speaking, the words sang into him, quenching a deep thirst. Conversation was the topic: how when a person speaks, they shouldn't only concentrate on their listener but be aware of what their own mind is doing. If everyone remained loyal to themselves, all tangles would loosen and harmony would reign.

So.

Aramani was the right place.

Aramani in the early hours.

Aramani during the morning class.

Because at those times it was impersonal. A set of ideas you could live inside. He had had his fill of relationships; wanted only the bare face of fate without interruption or comment, particularly from those like Alice, the woman who appeared to be interested in The Philosophy as something to be prodded and interrogated.

He was sorry when the class ended. He would have liked to sit for another hour, breathing in a peace, which for so many years he had taken for granted, but now came to him like an unbroken expanse of snow.

Outside, it was hot. Kasper stood for a moment on the steps that led down from the hall, his head light and uneasy. So, following an instinct that seemed as new to him as the outside world had once felt, he bent down, placing the palm of his hand on the stone. He was just beginning to register that his energy was moving more evenly through his body when he felt a tap on his shoulder.

Her again.

Alice.

'I'm leaving in three days if you want to write to Hanneke.'

At this he sat down, stared at her feet, planted sensibly on the step, her brown toes, the leather strap of her sandals...

'I must go,' he said.

By go he meant back to the peace of the swing or Yanna Lake or the silence of the high-up room. Now Alice had interrupted, like someone talking when you're in the middle of remembering a song.

'It's odd but I like this place,' she said. And in her voice he didn't, as he'd expected, hear Amsterdam but the silence of snow, the swing, the high-up place.

'It's the atmosphere. It's so clear. I've never felt more able to think as myself.'

'As yourself?'

'Yes. As myself when I'm not doing a job.'

'But that's just what you're doing here, isn't it – a job!'

'The job isn't as important as the person doing it, surely?'

And her face had the eerie softness that Kasper had seen on the faces of the residents when he had arrived in Aramani at the age of seven.

'I mean the job is important and I know that in doing it I've upset you, I really do know that. But I'll never forget Aramani. And don't forget the letter, if you want to write one, that is.'

When she had gone, Kasper's thoughts sped up in a movement so physical that he had to crouch down again on the step. And his stance returned him to London, to the day he and Surya had sat in the car and Surya had told him about his mother. After that, he could remember nothing but the horror of the post office closing.

And Christmas.

After his first two years in Aramani where Western festivals were all but ignored, nine-year-old Kasper began repressing his memory of their pleasures. With the effort of that distancing behind him, he was furious that in London, Christmas so forcefully demanded his attention, customers crowding into the post office with their packages and cards, as if warding off disaster.

As it happened, it was Surya who was facing disaster.

As usual, they went to his church for the Christmas service. With its fretted domed ceiling and plush seating, it was a place Kasper had always found baffling. Blind to the connection between the gold of the temple near Aramani and the grandeur of this church's interior, he wondered what could possibly be achieved by sitting in such a place. There was no real holiness to it that he could see, no light. The words made no sense. Any power there was seemed to emanate from the layered heaviness of the priests' embroidered robes, while in Aramani all precious things were outdoor and light and made of air.

When Surya went up to take Mass, Kasper's attention shifted from criticism to concern. The old man was moving awkwardly, arms held like two steadying sticks tight to his sides. With strange sounds being intoned, silver chalices raised, wiped with white linen and set down in a choreographed dance of the hands, Kasper focused only on his father. He heard the word blood and his mind leapt back to Amba's coloured water, and he imagined the liquid tipped to people's lips changing colour according to what they needed for healing. With past and present held so fast in opposition, a spasm of worry caused an audible snap in his head. So frightening was the sensation that he found himself leaping from the pew to which Surya had just returned and walking fast up the aisle.

A large man, sashed and adorned, placed his hand

on Kasper's head in blessing. Feeling, as so often, that he was in danger of breaking, Kasper slapped his own hand on the priest's and pressed hard. The priest sailed away, his billowing arms raised, mouth freshly intoning. Kasper already knew that the service had a script, but the child inside him hoped that in the face of such anguish it might for a second be dropped and real words spoken.

51

On Boxing Day, as they sat down to lunch, Kasper noticed that Surya looked unusually pale. At first, he attributed it to the closure of the post office and the stresses of his father's medical condition. He didn't ask him what was wrong. In London he never asked and Surya didn't ask either. And the two men appeared to be more content this way, standing at a slight distance from each other.

As they ate, a slick-haired star on the TV screen swilled brandy round a glass that looked like the rose vases Kasper had seen in Aramani's kitchens. Then suddenly Surya bent forwards, dropped his plate to the floor and held his chest as if an electric current were running at speed around his body. The actor on screen continued with his swilling and drawling but his father could only make a few gasping sounds, until finally the struggle was too much. And with the dog shoving at his feet, his body went limp.

Kasper shooed the dog away, spoke his father's name, shook his shoulder to rouse him. But within seconds it was clear that a hospital was needed.

A yellow directory sat on the shelf above the TV. He flicked through it hopelessly. Hospitals, hospitals... hundreds of hospitals and the print so small he could barely decipher the letters. He dialled a number. No answer. And suddenly he knew this was the wrong thing to do, that there was a faster way. Yet all he could think of was what a child might think: that if you run into the street and call for help someone will surely come.

But it was Boxing Day, it was afternoon, the streets were dark and wet and empty. Not a single shop was open. Only the crude light of decorations and dimmed street lamps enabled him to see where he was as he walked fast, faster, then ran, crying out to no one.

By the time he returned, Surya was dead.

In shock at the frozen form before him, his thoughts became fluid and fast, for if the body was so unimportant and the soul so precious, why did death take the body and not leave the soul behind? And why was it that he was unable to touch the skin of the being before him, not even the arm which had held him with such love as he had returned to the pew only a day earlier; whose movements he had known so well: the smile, the flick of his hands, the ruffling of his fingers through the dog's fur, the sound of his relief as he lowered himself into his chair after supper? Daily gestures only, which had nothing to do with the possible depth of his real being.

Propelled as by a rush of water, these thoughts swept Kasper out of the room, moving him round and round the kitchen, into the bathroom, his father's room, then his own where he sat shivering on the edge of the bed. When he returned to the sitting room and finally made himself lift the weight of Surya's head, he saw that the man might as well have been asleep, the open-mouthed pose being the same as the one he assumed during his regular evening doze. And suddenly he remembered with shame the Dutch visitor to Aramani who had spoken about the death of her father and how both Hanneke and he had dismissed her so callously.

At six, Magda came with a gift, as she did every Boxing Day. It was one of the many small regularities that had kept Surya going. His daily cup of tea, weekly visit to church, monthly drive in his car, customers known by name, and Magda who had always treated him so warmly while she had no interest in Kasper whom he supposed she still regarded as an intruder.

All that happened after this catapulted him into an entirely new world: her calling the ambulance, his going with the body to the hospital, arriving amid a crowd of Christmas casualties, and watching as his father, still to his eyes alive although cold now and stiff, was covered in a long, blue cloth and wheeled away.

52

Back in the house, Magda was still there. Seeing her in the armchair, the dog at her feet, again she reminded Kasper of Banhi. But instead of Banhi's stabilising silence, she started up on a rambling monologue about her years working in the shop. Then her oldest brother's weakened sight, her sister-in-law's heart disease, her own swollen feet... All this, Kasper later realised, must simply have been the sum of her fear: that early death would afflict either her or the family on whom she relied.

That night, Kasper tried finally to befriend the dog, that animal whose very existence he had never quite understood. For who or what was this animal who had seemed for the time he had been in London to have watched him with such suspicion? The Philosophy taught that humans only reincarnate as humans. But what if, for being free of language, animals had a deeper understanding of people than people did of each other? He tried talking to the dog, even explaining, as to a child, where her master had gone. In an unexpected show of interest, the animal looked up at Kasper, eyes tender and warm. Then she raised a paw. Kasper felt the furred claws and grasped them in both hands, tears spilling down his cheeks.

The next morning Magda arrived with her husband.

'He will explain.'

And what he explained was how death had nothing to do with the washing of clothes or the scattering of petals on a lake; it was complicated; it kept you busy for days: waiting for the post-mortem, getting hold of the death certificate, planning the funeral...

When this stranger of a man started on the subject of the shop and what he might do with it, Kasper ordered him to be quiet; it was too soon to think about that, and anyway, which he didn't say, he had no interest in running any kind of shop. He only wanted to honour his father with a good funeral.

And be gone.

Magda asked him if Surya had told him about his uncle. He told her he had referred to him in passing and that he had a vague memory of an uncle from childhood but that he hadn't seen or heard of him for years.

Why hadn't he? Why hadn't they met? Shouldn't he have introduced him to any family he had? But as he thought about Surya, he saw how solitary he had been, how lonely. And it dawned on him how much he had grown not to love, but feel something akin to love for the generosity with which the old man had so welcomed his son back.

In the end, he found his uncle's address and number in an old exercise book in a cupboard under the telephone and the voice that answered his call was confident and strong and very English.

When he pitched up the next day, it was clear to Kasper that the man wasn't in the least like his brother; he was richer and more assured, shaking Kasper's hand warmly, walking about the flat, checking inside cupboards, behind doors, tapping walls, standing outside on the pavement, looking up at the masonry in wide, confident gestures of ownership. Perhaps that's why Surya hadn't introduced them? Perhaps he'd been ashamed or shy?

Luckily, he didn't want to stay; he was over from Amsterdam for a few weeks on business and had booked himself into a nearby hotel. He would help Kasper organise the funeral; it could be complicated and expensive – up to five or six thousand pounds. Kasper told him that he had no experience either of funerals or paying for them. In India, a person was burnt on a pyre.

The awkwardness he felt at such ignorance must have caused a look of helplessness on his face for his uncle told him not to worry, that he was also aware of Kasper's story, reminding him that it was he who had told Surya that Kasper was in Amsterdam: 'a colleague of mine drops in on the studio from time to time.'

To this, Kasper remained silent, for dropping in on anyone, anything, seemed to him to represent the utmost of insults.

His uncle stayed in London on and off for ten days, and together they organised the service, the older man making the decisions but always with Kasper by his side. Catholic, as requested; even, unexpectedly, an open coffin, as if finally the man who had so shunned the limelight now wanted to be seen.

As his uncle was about to depart for the undertakers, Kasper said, 'He should wear these,' and handed him the brogues: those strange, stiff shoes which had travelled back and forth between India and England as if to represent the mysterious link between everyone in his life.

Once the coffin had been moved to the church, all night they sat. A handful of people came by to pay their respects: Magda and her husband, customers from the post office, a few men Kasper didn't know. Other than that, it was the two of them, alone with the candles, and a silence weighted in death and questions.

Where was Surya now? How could he lie there so ostentatiously in his coffin and yet not be in his body? And if he wasn't there, had he departed in one piece as one coherently organised being? Or was he scattered to a hundred different places: a habit lodged here, a memory lurking still in the post office, a part of him flown back to his childhood home in Goa...?

The rest of it was business: the funeral, the flat, the fact of the will leaving him nothing. Seeing his confusion, his uncle reassured him that he would give him a sum of money to make up for it. But as if his offer required repayment, he asked Kasper to speak more about India.

'What did you get out of such a sheltered existence?'

The question angered Kasper, implying as it did that possessions and land were the only things needed to make a life worthwhile, when Aramani was full of the spectacular, the strange.

'It was simple there. Profound. I operated the lift. Easy work but I learnt a lot about the mind and by the end I was teaching people from all over the world.'

'That's all very well for a young man. But you need to get yourself a proper job, earn some money at least, explore the real world.'

'Why?'

Kasper stared at this man as he scratched the huge muscle of his thigh.

'It's a shame you left school so young and didn't go to university. Still, I could help you, Kasper, I could give you work.'

'I don't want to work here.'

'I can take care of the flat, that's nothing, but you should think carefully about your future. This is a chance to start a new life.'

Again, he was irritated. Why was it that people outside Aramani saw the world only as a physical place with money as the measure of success? Why did nobody appreciate that the mind was also a world?

'If you don't want to stay here, why don't you go back to Amsterdam? By all accounts, you were beginning to make a good life there.'

Just what Surya had said. And he still had a connection to the place: the possibility of a child, someone who belonged to him...

But Hanneke! For Hanneke, he felt unreserved disgust.

It was late January when Kasper left London. And fewer than two days later, he was walking up through the village into Aramani's courtyard where Viraj sat in the afternoon sun.

As if nothing had changed.

Nothing had changed.

Nothing essential.

So what had come of it all?

This coming and going and staying?

There must be an end to the story, like the last word of a slogan, the correct returning of change on the post office counter or the bell of a London bus indicating the end of the journey.

53

Still seated on the step at the foot of the meditation hall, after the early morning class, Kasper thought of his brief spell in the world and concluded that he wanted nothing more from it: no journeys, adventures, no experiences beyond those he could find here. For all his attacks on it – its childishness, ill-conceived thinking and concealments – there was only here, only this power and the warm stone beneath his hand.

But how to stay?

But is the word that precedes an excuse.

It was also the word that made you grow up and for all he had suffered since his return, he realised now that it was a word with which he would have to make peace.

But *but* had never led to peace.

But Amba has changed, the buildings have changed, but Banhi isn't who I thought she was; there are things about The Philosophy I disagree with. I'm even unsure about God.

Finally he got up and, like someone trying to balance a pitcher of water on their head, he walked as slowly as he could back to his room, the space which had held him through these days of remembering.

Inside, he reached out to solid objects.

Had it not been so dusty, he would have lain his face against the stone floor. A thought stirred somewhere in his mind. It had worried him since his return that significant thoughts which had once guided him no longer seemed to form clearly or fast. Perhaps it was the fact of his having drunk alcohol? Perhaps he had damaged his brain or his soul. Or both? As a very young man, he could reach up so high to where the most delicate nuances added up to make meaning and so provide direction.

Now, instead of intuition, he used force:

I'll start my life again. Forget the word but. Stay. I will STAY.

Having made his decision, he wanted to be outside again. So without returning to the courtyard, he took pencils and sketchpad and walked the long road to Yanna Lake.

Seated on the bank, his glance turned to a young man, sleeves rolled up, fingers trailing across the surface of the water. The peace of the scene held him steady so that he moved a little closer and began sketching: long back, bent legs, the sinews of the arm, the palm of the hand cupping the cheek. When he reached the smooth side of the young man's neck, the lines of his drawing fell away.

Turn lust into creation.

With slogan as both shield and stick, he was suddenly filled with zest. He wouldn't go back to his room. Instead, he'd do a tour of Aramani in the way he had told the businessmen to. He would sit in all his favourite places and make a visual record of his love that would fix the place on paper, and so also his view of it.

He began with the front gates. Standing like the architect of a place he was about to redesign, he pencilled in the heavy black bars and the outline of the kitchen roofs visible above them. Then he moved to the courtyard, drew Viraj's empty chair, turned the page and went into the meditation room. A figure dozed in a corner. He stood just inside the doorway, lines appearing fast on the page. After that, he glanced at the low silver table in front of Gayan's vividly lit picture. On it stood a vase of real roses, packed tight and promising. These, he captured in a few swift strokes.

He became aware that he was hurrying, as if he knew that once the bell rang for mid-morning tea, people would emerge from all corners and the chance would be lost.

But I've got the rest of my life to draw Aramani.

His body had no sense of this thought, instead rushing him out of the room to the fruit store and another empty chair. Then Gayan's cane hut, to which he added hanging baskets and small seats, as well as a table and chairs, as if it were a proper house, but one that wasn't constructed in worldly ways, by means of money or unexpected connections with strangers, but by his own imagination.

269

There had been a stone urn on the balcony of Henry's shared house the first time he had stayed in Amsterdam. That, he brought into the picture too. He also included a Christmas tree, a car. Then he wrote the word brother in the middle of a blank page and on another the same word again, this time with a capital B as if the difference was the answer to a puzzle but also, for being only a letter of the alphabet, meant nothing at all.

He was walking at high speed now, his pad filling up. Finally, he decided he must take tea with everybody else. Never mind who was there – gossiping visitors or residents protecting their silence. Never mind either what kind of tea was served.

The tables were full. Three brothers wheeled in a trolley.

'What's going on?' His address was to the air.

'It's Wednesday,' a voice said.

In the past, being placed in time had upset him. Today it felt right to be reconnected to Aramani's routine: Wednesday, the day when they served the sweetly spiced chai he had been so used to drinking as a child.

Taking a cup from the wicker basket, he stood with the others in the queue, ready to find a table in the shade.

But once more his hands began shaking.

In a corner of the dining room, the residents gathered. In the past, they had taken tea to their rooms but on a Wednesday they had to line up like everyone else and, taught to serve, they waited until the visitors had had their share. Among them was Amba, laughing at words spoken beside him. Kasper watched him closely, the way his body leant into the group's as if it was made of the same material as that of the brothers he sat beside.

'A toast to the scooters!'

More laughter.

Then from nowhere, a scampering.

'Get him!'

In and out of the tables Amba darted wildly, until he reached the edge of the awning where there was a long trough for washing dishes. 'Ra ra ra!' he yelled. He waved then turned to smile at his audience. The scampering grew louder, a monkey finally landing on his back. Amba twirled round, leant forwards and jumped into the air as if trying to throw himself over the dining room wall to the cold stone below. And the monkey leapt with him onto a table, stuck its hand into a bowl of dried corn flakes and bounced away.

Kasper watched with fascination. He was suddenly a child again and here was his friend and with him a scooter and a ride into the mountains and love. He would have gone over to him, sat with him, talked, laughed...

But the energy of the scene was enough.

Soon he would be a part of it all again. He wouldn't sit at a table alone. He would move beside them as brother and equal, make his efforts modest and natural and live the stretching-up life with less pride. That's where he'd gone wrong; tried to run too fast, lost his breath, his balance, been caught out. Amba lived like an animal, Aramani written into his body, while for Kasper the place was a garment he wore tightly, then had to shed for the choking it caused. So he would change. He would no longer avoid what was ordinary. There would be monkeys and food and the seasons and the monsoons. There would be running from one room to another for shelter, and the annoyance of wet clothes. He would visit Banhi, too, and sit with her in silence and help Amba with his coloured water and do whatever job he was given, even if it meant being back in the darkened hall, scraping vegetables.

He found himself adding image after image to the life he intended. Sketchpad closed, he looked out once more at the mountains, the khejri trees below and the road stretching beyond the iron back gates that led to the village where the bangle-seller was, the tailors, the cows and perhaps another donkey. He would go there too from time to time, if only to take in the colour and ease.

He had tried to live a monochrome life, even cut out the colour of the sky and the purple of the bougainvillea, scrubbed himself clean, taking bath after bath, as if wanting to wash off his own skin. He would no longer do that. He would wear the flesh of Aramani, the whole mountain, the community, the villagers, the dhobi, the animals. And the monkeys. He would jump in the air with Amba and shoo them away but also throw them bread so that he could get close to them, feel their twitching and leaping and allow himself to be surprised.

'Kasper!'

He looked up.

Alice.

Again!

'I thought you didn't like our tea.'

'I'm having this.' She held up a teabag. Associating her only with Hanneke, he expected it to be herbal, but a small tag hung from it: PG Tips. The tea his father had drunk daily.

'I've been looking for you.'

'Well, here I am.'

'What are those?'

'Drawings.'

'Of?'

'Does it matter?'

'Who's that?'

She pointed to the sketch of the young man lying beside Yanna Lake.

'No one. It's no one.'

His breathing became shallow; he was unable to swallow.

'What's going on?' he gasped, as if he knew he was about to be woken when all he wanted was to turn over and rest.

'Kasper, I need to be honest with you.'

'No you don't. What you need to do is go away!'

He could feel her plucking up courage and he wanted to shove her, as Raj had shoved him as a child.

Raj.

What had happened to Raj, that boy who had such mixed-up feelings about Aramani that he felt he needed both to protect and destroy it at the same time?

'Go on then,' he said, aware of his curtness and how different it was from the way one was meant to speak here.

Meant to, instructed to, required to.

'What is it?'

'A tissue of lies.'

The word tissue was as light in her voice as the swish of the muslin curtain that hung from Gayan's door.

She said it again. This time, the word *lies* fell upon him like the weight of a large meal.

273

'I've been talking to the couple who've befriended you. Mina and Balvan. We met in the hotel. They live in Holland. Balvan is a business friend of your uncle's.'

'How do you know my uncle?'

'I don't. I know nothing about him other than that as soon as he found out you'd come here instead of Amsterdam, he contacted Balvan. He—'

'Balvan?'

'Yes, Balvan goes to the studio in Amsterdam from time to time.'

'And you tell me now rather than when you first met me! Just before you leave. Doing your research, getting the best out of Aramani, then wrecking my life and disappearing!'

'It's not that simple. You might be interested to know that I'm in the middle of a divorce, a bad one, so yes it's true I've taken strength from Aramani but that doesn't mean it's perfect, the word you reacted against so strongly in our first conversation, if you remember? Anyway, your uncle was trying to protect you, Kasper. He wanted you to get proper work, not return here and spend your life in a lift. Balvan was coming to India on business so your uncle asked him-'

'Business! I detest business. It gets into everything. What is business, in fact? Just money! I'm sorry about your divorce.'

Kasper pictured his uncle again, not seeing him as a man who might have felt a genuine responsibility for his nephew, but recalling him only as a lawyer, foraging for evidence.

He looked up at Alice. The fringe, the blue eyes, intelligent face...

'So why are you here really? Apart from to recover from your divorce?'

'I've told you. To find out more about the place. How it makes people suffer.'

'So you decided in advance that it makes people suffer! And yet you've enjoyed it here.'

Fury again. She was telling the truth. At least about herself. And the truth was an obstacle he had been trying to avoid. For each time he felt he was beginning to find his way, there she was again, facing him with words he didn't want to hear.

'Yes, I've been surprised by what I've felt while being here. But a place can be two things, in fact many things at once. Can't it?'

'No!'

And yet he had been feeling the same himself.

'And Mina and Balvan are nothing to do with the lift being renovated in case you were wondering.'

'How did you know I was thinking that?'

'You don't have a monopoly on telepathy.'

'I really wish you'd leave me alone.'

She looked up at him and smiled.

'I'm sorry. I didn't mean that.'

'It doesn't matter.'

He sensed suddenly that there was something much graver that mattered and that he should walk away from her right now. But he knew if he did, she would always be with him, if not in person, then in his mind.

He opened his sketchbook again, stroked the head of the boy he had drawn, in the way he should have liked his own head to be stroked, as a child who is loved not coerced. Finally, he began to calm down as if the very texture of the paper were clothing that protected.

'Who's that?'

'You just asked that. I don't know. Someone I saw at the lake.'

Again, a wave of foreboding. Like a patient facing an operation that has been postponed over and over until it can no longer be avoided. All this dithering and rushing and changing his mind had been because of the fear of the needle and the incisions to follow.

I have made my decision and that's it. I will never leave Aramani again. Never.

The tea urns were wheeled away. Residents left first, then guests, some wishing to continue conversations, to talk about the problem of their minds. He suddenly felt furious with Aramani's visitors. Why not *do* something? Have children, distract themselves, instead of walking around in pyjamas, endlessly picking at their thoughts? But it was himself he was cross with because that was precisely what he was guilty of. And while he had been overthinking, others had been busy behind his back.

Again, she started up.

'Listen, Kasper. I haven't come here to hurt you. But there's one thing that Hanneke talked to me about after you'd left Holland.'

He got up to go.

'Your mother.'

'What about her?'

'She worked for Viraj. Did you ever wonder about that?'

Still standing, as if coming up for air, his eyes once more sought the mountains.

'Didn't you ever wonder why you were brought here at such a young age? Why you were given the welcome you were, why you were privileged above the other residents?'

'I worked hard.'

'Of course.'

He hated her patronising voice.

'The man you lived with in London wasn't your father, Kasper. That's what I came here to tell you.'

'She told you that! Hanneke?'

He spat out the name as if delivering a blow to Alice's face.

'And you wanted me to *write to her*? Don't tell me anymore.'

'Kasper. Please. It'll come out in the end. Don't you think you should be the first to be told?'

'*Me* the first to know when you say you know about it all already, whatever *it* is?'

Frustration filled his head like a furious itch, as it had as a boy when he had wanted to draw but had been summoned to run an errand instead.

'I've been recovering too.'

'And?'

'Only that Hanneke always knew. She loved you but she also knew that you were the child of someone here. She loved Aramani as much as you.'

'That's hard to believe.'

'She did. She never stopped talking about it. And when she guessed you were the child of an Elder, you took on an extra patina.'

'How do you expect me to understand that word? *I left school at seven.* You knew that as well, no doubt.'

'I'm sorry. Glamour. Attraction. You had an attraction.'

'And so she stole me. As if I was an object, a trinket like the stuff you people buy from the kiosk. To take home. A souvenir. An original, inscribed with the name of an Elder! This whole business, everything that's happened is her fault. She's a thief! And a liar!'

'She's not a liar, Kasper.'

'But she *is* a thief!'

'We should go to the hotel. They'll be waiting.'

'Who will?'

'Mina and Balvan.'

'Oh them. Well, let them wait! Since *I've been waiting my whole life!*'

54

Once more, Mina was seated by the pool. Kasper imagined her peering through a pair of binoculars, reporting back to Balvan one or another indiscretion.

Just as he was thinking this, she turned and smiled warmly. This confused him, as if everyone was changing, everything moving at such a pace that he was becoming several people at once in the same way that they were. For a second, he expected to see a monkey landing on the table and turning into his mother or Hanneke or one of her children or this Dirk of hers.

'Kasper. Alice. Sit down. Balvan is off somewhere. We won't wait for him.'

'I'll stand,' said Kasper, although his head was spinning and he knew he needed something to hold on to.

'I brought Kasper here so you could confirm what I've just told him. About his father.'

'Your uncle in London asked us to give you this letter, Kasper. He found it when he was clearing out Surya's flat after you left. It was never posted.'

Another letter not delivered, another outpouring of grievances, complications, questions...

'Why didn't you tell me all this before?'

'We love this place, that's why. We wanted to take

refreshment from the atmosphere.'

'But you think Aramani's an illusion. How can you refresh yourself on an illusion? You can't have it both ways. Why don't you just get out of here!'

He knew he was talking to himself as much as to the two women before him.

'Wherever you go, however good a place, it will always have its troubles. Our house needs new drains.'

'What?'

Kasper stared at this great nuisance of a woman, disgusted by the comparison she had just drawn.

'You need to read the letter.'

'I need to read all the letters!'

'Never mind that. Here.'

So she was the surgeon, knife raised ready to cut. It was what he'd been waiting for: the cold of the blade then the pain. And after it, finally… the knowing, the truth. The Philosophy was wrong about truth and pain having nothing to do with each other. Alice was right. They went hand in horrible hand, everywhere, through everything.

> *One day the sun will explode, the earth crack and*
> *nature will rebel. You are here to prepare for that.*

But you had to be perfect first.

> *Live only in the light, don't ask any questions, be*
> *obedient, say yes. Say: I will do whatever you ask…*

'I told you that Mina and Balvan are friends of Surya's brother. They came here to help you.' Alice spoke carefully.

Still Kasper didn't turn.

'So, I repeat: why now? Why wait until today to spill all your beans?'

'We wanted to get to know you a little.'

'*Why?* The letter was addressed to me. You should have delivered it immediately.'

Then a hand on his shoulder. Mina again, as tall and huge as the Elders had seemed when he was a child: those mountains of sari, folded round and around them until there seemed nothing of flesh to their bodies at all.

She held his arm and led him to a chair.

'Forgive us. Here. The letter.'

He recognised his father's thin handwriting slanting to the right as if pushed over; the same writing he had seen day after day in the post office, on Christmas and birthday cards. Birthdays which weren't celebrated in Aramani.

When he was seven, Kasper had counted the hours until January the twelfth, the day when in London he had always woken with excitement, because there would be gifts and love; a party and friends. But on that first January, eleven months after their arrival in Aramani, his mother had sat him down and told him that he was a soul not a body and that the soul went on forever so it didn't have a birthday. Made for joy, he had somersaulted his disappointment into excitement, as if he was the only soul in the world and, for not being a body, everyone else was ordinary. Then she said that his birthday fell on the same day as Aramani's and there was always a big celebration that day which he could take part in and think of as his own.

'So places not people have birthdays?'

As he looked down at the letter Mina had handed him, the memory rose up in him differently now. The

281

paper, folded in several different ways, had the look of a message that had passed through many hands.

My dear brother

He wondered why his father who they were saying wasn't his father didn't use his brother's name. As if they were strangers or far from each other in age, or not brothers at all?

I am very grateful for your enquiries. The fact that you have been able to talk directly to some of these people in India is a comfort. I knew already of course about Kasper's real father. Before she died, Yasmin described him. The fellow she worked for in Aramani.

Now she has gone, I have lost the will to hunt Kasper down and bring him back. If he ever returns, I will of course look after him, but by all accounts, he is quite happy where he is.

Of course, if you find out any further information, please pass it on.

Kindly,

Surya

They watched as he read.
'Why didn't he tell me this himself?'
'I don't know,' said Alice. 'But you see what you have to do, Kasper. Go to Viraj. Face him.'

Kasper's mind was in London. All that time, those evenings, those spaces of silence in which Surya could have spoken, and so saved him the *buts* and the joy of return. But there had never been silence, there had been an incessant flow of talk and always in the background, the sound of the TV, that stupid means of distraction that takes a man's mind away from the point of the knife and the pain.

'You're as bad as each other. You have nothing to do with me. Either of you. You're just visitors. You should go home and forget about Aramani.'

'Kasper, it doesn't matter about us. But you matter. Like I said, go to Viraj. Face him!' Alice's voice was gentle.

'And you really think he'll tell me?'

'I don't know. But he'll know that you know and that's the important thing. It's a chink in their armour.'

'Why do you care about their armour? Apart from the fact that you're doing some kind of research project?'

'We care about truth, Kasper. Just as you do.'

He got up; Alice, too. She shook Mina's hand, took Kasper by the shoulders and walked him away.

'Thank you for trusting me,' she said, as if the operation were over and he was back in the ward, sleepy but healed.

At this he pulled away. Steadied himself into a fast walk and returned through the gates to the courtyard where he came to a stop.

Some years ago, when the first guests from abroad had begun visiting, there had been a brother from Japan, very tall and white in his kurtas, who had come to just such a standstill in the courtyard. Nobody could move him. People tried talking to him, but he remained silent, his eyes wide open and staring until two of the larger residents had to push him to the ground and carry him like a log to his room. Later, Kasper heard he had been committed to an asylum.

I must move.

55

But where to? He wasn't ready to face Viraj. Nor did he want to go back to his room. Again, his feet knew. Those size nine feet, narrow and strong. Out of the back gates again, up the hill to the village, through the gap in the wall, down the hill, a left turning past the tailor's, the hardware stores, the bags of rice and lentils, the stainless steel dishes and cups, the children in their bright dresses, until he reached the bangle-seller's shop.

The evening before he had left Aramani with Hanneke, it was to the bangle-seller he had gone, taking with him the letters wrapped in newspaper, tied with cord from an old pair of kurta bottoms.

'Will you do something for me?' he had asked. 'Would you keep these somewhere safe? It's just a few papers.'

'A few? There must be a thousand papers here!'

'I don't know how many but I don't want to take them with me. It was a story I was writing but I didn't know how to end it so I want to leave it here. I'm going away for a while. If I had any money I'd pay you, but I only have this.' And he had handed the bangle-seller a notebook. 'Maybe your son could use it.'

The bangle-seller told him to keep his notebook, his son preferred football to books.

'I'll put your bundle here,' he said, pointing to a shelf filled with papers.

'Thank you.' And at the time, Kasper had thought it was God speaking through the man's smile, telling him he was doing the right thing in entrusting the letters to the bangle-seller. Now he was back in Aramani, he had thought vaguely that if he ran away again he would leave the letters where they were; if he stayed, he would have plenty of time to fetch them. And by then, after all his practice reading with Lars in Amsterdam and then London, he would be able to decipher their wording.

He was sweating as he approached.

Inside, the bangle-seller sat opposite a small boy, pointing to something the child had written. Kasper heard his laughter, watched the man pat the boy on the head, the boy smile, take a sweet from a plate on a stool beside him and make another attempt at what he was doing, pressing his pencil hard down on the paper on his lap. About them hung rail upon rail of goods for sale. Not just bangles but earrings, necklaces, charm bracelets, scarves...

Kasper longed for the feel of them, longed to be swathed in soft cloth, weighted by jewels, even to be the boy, so held in family affection.

'Hello?' Voice, hollow and quiet.

The bangle-seller stood up, patting his son's head again as a signal that he should continue what he was doing and do it carefully.

'Liftman! I heard you were back. How are you? Look how my business has blossomed and my boy is writing now, not just playing football! Your package must have brought us luck. All the Westerners come here first before they go near the other shops! So I made it into an altar. He lifted up a small statue of Lakshmi, orange flowers draped about her neck, the letters her stand.

The bangle-seller smiled. Like Surya, he had a tooth missing.

Kasper stared.

His father.

Who wasn't his father.

> *Always remember you have three fathers. God the father, Gayan your spiritual father and the father of your body.*

'That's what I came for. The package. I'd like it back.'

'Of course. But without it my business –'

'Everyone's business seems to have blossomed. Everything new. So many buildings, people…'

'Yes, the mountaintop has blossomed. And now my son is blossoming. He pointed to the boy's notebook. He can even do quadratic equations!'

Kasper dismissed the confusion he felt at this cameo of contentment.

'I need to take the package. Now! I have to go.'

The bangle-seller tapped the side of his nose then held out his hand.

'You want money? You just said the letters, I mean the package, helped you make money? I haven't got any money. You don't have money if you live in Aramani. It's only the visitors who have money.'

'But you don't live in Aramani anymore.'

Fury tightened his chest. Why was it only money that

made people speak or keep quiet? It seemed you even had to pay for someone to smile.

'I was joking!' The bangle-seller laughed and seeing another customer approach he let Kasper go.

56

In the dining room, Elders talked while they ate. Kasper took his seat beside Viraj, watched the man's elegant fingers tear off a corner of chapatti, gather into it rice and dhal, then deftly fold it into his mouth; watched, too, as he dabbed his face to check it was clean.

That he might have kissed his mother.

That he would have touched her as gently.

That he was his son!

He tried not to think of it, to tend instead to his own eating. Deliberately he was clumsy, scooped up too much for one mouthful then messily slurped on his buttermilk.

Food spilt as his mouth spilt words.

'Viraj, I need to talk to you.'

'I rest after lunch.'

'It's important.'

'In that case, of course.'

Kasper waited ten minutes before walking up the stairs to Viraj's room and sat, resting his back against the warm wall of the building, palms flat against the stone. He wished he could drop off for just a few moments.

But there was no time.

Footsteps sounded beneath him, and looking down, he saw the sister who had been in the dining room the day before he'd delivered his talk in the new auditorium and then had been paraded by Mina before the audience of vast public men. At first, he could find no words although he longed to ask her if she realised she was being 'exploited' for her youth and good looks. Alice's words, and the right ones too. He told himself firmly not to be distracted. But when it was she who spoke, telling him warmly that her name was Priti and that she worked for Viraj, he suddenly saw his mother repeated: as beautiful and about the same age as she'd been when she had first visited Aramani. Then he thought of himself again and stated in a question, 'but you're like me, you're not fully Indian.'

'No, my mother was Spanish. She brought me here when I was three.'

'Why didn't I know you? I was a child here too.'

'You were older than me. Anyway I went to school in the village.'

'You went to school?'

'Yes. They thought we should continue our education. At the senior school in the village.'

'I thought there was only a school for small children in the village.'

'No? There was a senior school too. Small. Near the bank.'

By this he was baffled. Had she learnt to read novels, write essays, decipher scientific ideas? *Do quadratic equations?* Why hadn't he been to school too? Was it because they regarded his role as so special that The Philosophy was enough? Or was it to deprive him of the very skills he would need in order to subject Aramani to proper scrutiny?

Seeing his preoccupied face, Priti turned her back and, leaving the door open, went into Viraj's room. As if she were taking him with her, he stared as she sat at the desk, wishing he had the time and peace of mind to draw the very small bed, chair, wardrobe, the two desks, one for Viraj, one for Priti. It looked so clean, so much as he had imagined it. But a glance at Viraj as he climbed the steps told Kasper that the man in London who wasn't his father had it right about the pressure Viraj had exerted on his mother. For his dismissal of Priti was as sharp as his gesture to Kasper to enter his room. Inside, he adjusted the already spotless bedding, straightened Priti's chair, put the papers she had started working on into a drawer then opened the shutters. Sun flooded the space so that Kasper could barely see.

'So, my brother, what can I do for you?'

Kasper looked at him and was at a loss. During his whole time in Aramani, he had never seen Viraj at such close quarters. He had always been walking away or disappearing into a room. Now, Kasper wondered if this wasn't his way, too, of avoiding scrutiny.

'You should never have left Aramani.'

'I didn't choose to be here.'

'You were meant to be here. Gayan says –'

'I don't want to know what Gayan says. I want to know what you say.' Kasper slammed his hand down on the desk.

Viraj remained calm, as if he had created an atmosphere that cut short dissent.

'We should go for a walk, Viraj.'

'I have no time for walking. We can speak on the balcony.'

As Kasper followed Viraj outside, he had the feeling that this was one of the most important moments of his life; he must take hold of it fast.

'Viraj,' he said, before he had even accepted the seat offered. 'My mother came here when she was a young married woman. She worked for you. Seven years later she returned, bringing me with her and leaving her husband behind in London.'

Kasper looked up at the sky, trying to find words of his own, not quotes from a letter or from Alice.

'Children don't usually stay here. But I was allowed to stay here because you were my father.'

There. He had said it and put it in the past tense. There was no present in this relationship.

Viraj stood up.

'You've got everything muddled.'

'So you're not going to tell the truth.'

'I care more than anything that you strengthen your spirit, Kasper.'

'Ah, like a true Indian father, you *care for my achievements*. And I fulfilled them. All the time I lived here, I worked hard. But I never went to school. I never learnt what normal children learn. I never learnt Maths like your Priti did! I couldn't even read properly! *I'm still learning to read!* And yet you taught me that I didn't have to read anything to become one of the best souls in the world! *Why?*'

Hearing himself speak these words which would, after all, make no sense to any rational human being, his legs became stiff, in the way they had just before he had kicked Raj as a child. Raj! Yes, what about Raj? Had he been to school?

Then suddenly he lost the will to assert himself.

'Not that I minded. Not then. I loved it here. I had Amba. I had you. I followed you. Watched every move you made and copied you. You were a good teacher.'

'Don't become attached, Kasper.'

Viraj moved close to him but Kasper placed the palm of his hand on the man's chest and pushed him away hard so that suddenly this model of excellence and beauty looked very small.

'I couldn't be attached to you if I tried. But that doesn't mean I'm not your son. Why would the man who I thought was my father have told a lie like that? We must go for a walk, Viraj. To Yanna. And you can tell me what you used to think about when you took your daily stroll around the lake in the way I copied. All those times when you were meant to be thinking about The Philosophy! But you weren't, were you! You were thinking about my mother! Or Priti's mother! Or Priti even! And you didn't even shed a tear when Mama died! When I went to London, Surya told me she was ill. Is that why she was sent away? Because people are a nuisance if they're ill? *Why didn't you look after Mama?* You make sure Banhi is looked after! *Is it because she wasn't Indian?*' His voice trembled as he spoke these last words.

'None of this is true, Kasper. Someone's been lying to you. People are always lying about Aramani –'

'*In* Aramani. People lie *in* Aram-'

'Kasper. Stop! I cared for you, but I. Am. Not. Your father.'

'Why aren't you?'

They were the words of a child, confused to the very core.

'So, I'm on my own now. There's nobody here.'

'Nobody is on their own.'

'Everyone is on their own, Viraj. Everyone who isn't fully Indian. And everyone with a secret. So you especially!'

As Kasper walked down the stairs, he met Priti again. She was smiling, as if someone had told her something funny. The sun shone on her black hair and the sparkling white teeth of her smile made Kasper ache for what she was.

By six, the courtyard was cold. A light rain fell – the first since his return. Kasper thought again of the brother from Japan who was now in an asylum, and decided to take shelter in the meditation room.

Seated on the white-sheeted floor, he looked yearningly into Gayan's eyes; those eyes he had punctured with his fist so many years ago and were now mended, as artificial things can always be mended.

His thoughts wandered as he sat; to Viraj, then Mina, Alice, the bangle-seller; Banhi, blind and unaware. At the thought of her his mind quietened, it suddenly occurring to him that it was just possible that she was the only one who might know the whole story. Then he switched scenes again, this time to Surya lying in his coffin, his mother, his future, Hanneke... Everything but the very silence that this room was made for.

In a desperate bid for calm, he moved from the floor to the single chair at the back of the room which was reserved for those who no longer had the strength to sit unsupported. And as if the raised position or the power of the chair itself had come to his aid, finally he began to slow down. And suddenly he was back in the high room, then somewhere even higher than that: the sky, the space above the sky, to peace and a place of acceptance.

For the first time in days, everything was still, everything positioned. All questions silenced. He sat on, his back finally relaxing, as if someone had thrown open the windows and let in the breeze and it was softly warm and a part of his own breathing.

This was the Aramani he loved. The silent Aramani that had a beauty and calmness best felt if you closed your eyes. But you weren't meant to close your eyes. Yet if you did, you could feel the air on your face, picture the kites, the early mornings, the stored pictures in your mind – Aramani without the crushing, betraying, deadening structure that held it together.

But as soon as he was out in the cool air again, the door to the high room slammed shut and he was left with one question. The question he had asked his mother when he was a small boy:

> *Why talk to a picture when Gayan is only a few yards away?*

57

Gayan.

It was the name he had spent years trying to push to the edge of his consciousness yet the name that had come to him in Amsterdam, London, on buses, trains, planes, dreams… The name that had always made him feel guilty and yet the name he had never stopped saying out loud in times of trouble. And wasn't this the most troubling moment of his life and so the very time to ask him for help?

As a child, Kasper had never made special preparations to see Gayan. It was his mother who'd been the fussy one, fiddling and brushing her hair over and over, smoothing her sari before she went to the old man's cottage. In his teenage years, he, too, had scrubbed himself clean before visiting his teacher, wanting Gayan to see him only in the best light, refreshed and well, and seated in his high room.

Now he was none of those things.

But he didn't care.

It was time to see him in person.

'Kasper, come in.'

The words made him jump. By the time he had recovered himself, Gayan had drawn the curtain back and was standing before him. And with the conviction that there was no one in the world left to trust, Kasper's courage returned. He looked into Gayan's eyes and together they stood in a silent salute. No combat, no barrier. Instead, another new truth. Then a light. Different from the one that could so fill a room that it blinded you to what was happening within it. This was a harshly revealing light, a torch against skin, showing up every pore, every hair... As if Gayan were peeling a mask from his features to reveal someone different. And that someone wasn't a holy man, a teacher or leader, but all of those and none – which was exactly what Kasper had always dreaded him being.

Apart from a small plastic oval in each bathroom, mirrors were forbidden in Aramani. But Europe was full of them. Kasper had seen himself over and over, from all angles: in shop windows, car windows, glass doors, hall mirrors, bathroom mirrors, bedroom mirrors. He had come to know his own features well... And now they were repeated before him: the same nose, the same determined jawline, eyelashes thick and black.

Here was his father.

It was suddenly as obvious as the khejri trees repeating themselves on the road that led to the village. How could he possibly have not seen it before? At least, not suspected, when it seemed to him now that everyone else must have known?

His mind slipped and slipped until he felt light-headed. He wanted to hate yet there was only the need to keep looking. And this time, something else danced across Gayan's features: a plea so subtle as almost to be imperceptible, not from him but from the holiness he claimed to inhabit him.

Forgive him.

The thoughts travelled between them in silence. And for that, the unspoken exchange was one of the pinnacles of Kasper's spiritual life. During the long seconds that he stood still, he understood perfectly:

Any man can fall.

But as if compassion had visited him like a kite darting past, suddenly its opposite came. Rage. For if you go on and on about how you are inhabited by holiness, if you sit in your room while everyone else does the work, if you give lecture after lecture pinning people to your every word, if you interrupt just when a person is doing what they most love: painting, walking, climbing Jagar Rock, being rowed across Yanna Lake; if you click your fingers and expect everyone to be at your feet the moment it suits you and send them away when it doesn't, then what are you are, in the end?

A dictator!

And if you say that those who clean the latrines are untouchable and yet you want your own latrine cleaned, what are you?

A hypocrite!

His gaze turned to the silver cup by Gayan's side.

Mahua flowers.

Oh yes?

And with that question, suddenly the moment of sacredness which might have saved all he had learnt and stored and treasured was broken.

He went over to the silver cup and drank it down in one.

'Kasper! Stop! *Stop NOW!*'

'Why? You drink it! Why shouldn't I?'

But he hadn't reckoned on the strength of the liquid the silver cup contained. Whatever it was, it was sweet, and yet in seconds his head was spinning.

'You shouldn't have done that!'

'Nor should you!'

And that was it, Kasper dropped everything he had ever held dear, climbed onto the bed, stretched up to the prints of Bombay, ripped them from the wall, shouting at Gayan that he didn't understand why he should enjoy such stuff when everyone else was stuck with *those stupid cartoons!*

'I love art. I have loved it all my life.'

Still on the bed, Kasper stared at him, astonished.

But he pressed on.

'So you had the paintings in that new auditorium done by an artist from outside!'

Silence.

'Hanneke. She painted them, didn't she! They look like hers. Did you pay her? Do you know her well? How did you communicate with her?'

And in a moment of comically perfect timing, not unusual in Aramani, the phone rang. Kasper ran to it, put his hand over the receiver, Kala gabbling into his palm, and yanked the wire from the wall then kicked the table, pushed over the chairs, yelled at Gayan that it was *his wife* on the phone, that he was a liar, a fraud, that Hanneke was as bad, weren't the pictures infused with her greed, her *lust*, had he made his request to her over the *this* (here he held up the handset that looked like something from a grotesque form of doll's house.) *Had he slept with her too?* At this, Gayan stood up fast, his hand raised to hit. But Kasper was a car with no brakes, no driver.

'And while we're sorting things out, why did you make me responsible for the letters when you knew I couldn't read? Why didn't I go to school? Why did you let me go to Amsterdam when you knew I would suffer? You say you're my father. You are *no father!*'

It was beyond him to mention his mother. She shouldn't be spoken of in this room where –

No!

58

As if he had expressed every one of his thoughts out loud, Gayan's voice sounded from a distance. Swaying now, Kasper heard the sharpness. He also knew what would come next: he'd be arrested and taken away, locked up.

So, upset yet exhilarated, he made a run for it, kicking the muslin curtain aside, pelting unsteadily up the hill, his chappals slapping against the hot road.

In his room, he turned once more to the package he had collected from the bangle-seller, pulled at the cord until the letters fell out in heaps. He looked at the different types of handwriting, skim-reading odd paragraphs as he went. Finally, he divided them up, and in an attempt to restore order, gave each one its place so that his room became a dismantled book with no spine.

Stuck to a wall:

> *Gayan, I worked hard at school like you told me to. I had a scholarship to study in Chicago which I wrote to tell you about BUT I DIDN'T HEAR BACK FROM YOU. Anyway, my father told me it was a waste of time. By his reckoning, the world would be destroyed before the end of my second year of studying. If I'd disobeyed him, I'd have graduated by now and might*

*have a decent job. Do you know what I do now to earn
just enough to live with my parents? I load up fish vans
at our local port. What do you think of that?*

On the floor beside his desk:

*Dear Gayan I would like you to explain why it is that
the only things I am EVER asked to do are clean the
bathrooms and the garage. I don't even live in this
house. I have a bathroom of 'my own' to clean and
children to look after. They were born before I joined
Aramani. The woman you sent to look after the studio
here does nothing. She just tells other people to do
things for her. She doesn't have to work, she doesn't
have to earn money so why can't she clean the house
in all the spare time she has? One day I asked her and
she said that she had a lot on her mind and was busy.
As far as I can see, the only things she does is eat and
telephone people to ask them for money. I don't mention
her name here because you know who I'm talking
about.*

Across the other side of the room on the floor:

*Gayan – Yesterday I saw my father cry. He said: I'm so
worried about you. You're making yourself ill depriving
yourself of sleep to get up so early. You need more
protein in your diet, more exercise.
I have NEVER seen my father cry, ever. I was so
shocked because I thought I was looking well and
clean in my white sari. He said: YOU LOOK LIKE A
MADWOMAN! Gayan, you said doubts would come.*

> *But now I'm beginning to wonder if my father isn't*
> *right. Also my mother joined The Philosophy so he is*
> *upset about that. He has lost both of us. Please reply. I*
> *have written twice…*

At this letter, twice written, twice ignored, Kasper burst into tears. His head was splitting now with a terrible pain. He went into the bathroom, turned on the tap and doused his face in cold water before forcing himself to return to the room.

On his bed:

> *Gayan, I am writing this from the school where I have*
> *been teaching for eight years. The journey takes over an*
> *hour and the traffic is bad. Before that I have to attend*
> *two classes in two different places and change my*
> *clothes each time. Last week, I drove into the back of a*
> *lorry. It was because I was tired…*

Head still reeling from what he had drunk, Kasper rose unsteadily to his feet then without thought kicked the wall in fury.

At these words.

These terrible felt-words which might have been his own. Like blood, they rushed into his high room flooding the space he had spent his entire adult life working to preserve.

When he tried to move, a memory released itself of the taxi that had brought him back just over a month ago. The stink of asafoetida. The spice you couldn't taste when it was cooked but raw, in a sack that was split, made you vomit.

Just like Aramani.

So perfect, so beautiful and ordered. But once unpacked, a place where sorrows festered unacknowledged. The connection gave him strength to shove an arm out to one side and slide a last letter towards him.

> *I've been wanting to write to you for four months to say that I cannot express myself very well. It would be better to talk to you. But I can never put it into words. So I decided to keep it quiet. God settles it in the end, doesn't he? God makes it right?*

With this fragment, Kasper lay for a few seconds, the page close to his chest, astonished at the way his hand had hit on words that summed up most clearly what he himself so longed to believe. If in leaving he had betrayed Gayan, what did it matter? And if from the outset Gayan had betrayed him, what did that matter either?

But what to do with these terrible letters? How to honour them and yet be free of them too? They had nothing to do with him. Still, how could he have been so proud, so aloof, so ambitious, so gullible, so stupid, *cold*...?

More than ever, it was the cold he felt now.

59

At twenty minutes to ten, Kasper left his room. The teaching block would be empty. Everyone preparing for night, some on walks, others in their rooms, the residents dozing over unfinished work, reading, ironing... Little things for the coming, clean day.

Since the lift had been out of use, Kasper had visited the place daily. The last time had upset him. Everything had been removed, leaving only the lift shaft. As a boy, he would have found it fun to run up the stairs and peer into the darkness, calling his name in the hope of an echo. Now, with the letters close to his chest, he hated the thought of such emptiness.

Opening the door, he was faced by a litter of rubble, air full of dust. Still, he walked slowly up the stairs adjacent to the shaft. On the fifth floor, sensing he was about to sneeze, he pressed his nose hard to stop a sound that was too full of a past and a parent: Amba here and his mother in London. The shaft was a vertical drop beside him. He only had to climb over the railing that ran alongside the staircase, hold his breath, take a step, and jump. But he wanted to sit, as he had on Jagar Rock. Sit and sit, staring at the horizon, leaning further and further forwards until the sun slipped down to bring night.

It was his body that had led him to this place on the stair, as if the stair belonged only to him. He was very aware of his arms and legs which felt both heavy and terribly light. But it was the letters that screamed at him for they summed up both his guilt and all that he wished he had grown into: a being who could understand, who had the power to fight for compassion and justice. This thought at least was clear. And after all the confusion, the physical act would be easy. With the letters clutched to his chest, falling would be easy.

Any man can fall.

It was climbing that was hard.

ACKNOWLEDGEMENTS

With my heartfelt thanks to Keir Alexander, Flo Bender, Aidan and Nancy Chambers, Lucinda Drayton, Frances Hedgeland, Andrew Hogg, Emma Innes, Anna Jacobs, Ray Kilby, Kathryn Lloyd, Jasmine Murray, Harriet Distefano, Susie Nott-Bower, Eugene Romain, Rowena Rolt, John Seal, Kai Smith, Marneta Viegas, and all unnamed others who have helped in the composing of words that have required such delicate handling.

Milton Keynes UK
Ingram Content Group UK Ltd.
UKHW010829190224
438095UK00004B/182

9 781739 254957